BAD MONKEY

BAD MONKEY

stories

Curtis Smith

Press 53
Winston-Salem, NC

Press 53
PO Box 30314
Winston-Salem, NC 27130

First Edition

Cover design by Kevin Watson

Cover photo copyright © 2009 by Murray Ballard and Angus Dunican

Printed on acid-free paper

ISBN: 978-0-9824416-5-7

To my parents

We are accustomed to look upon the shackled form of a conquered monster, but there—there you could look at a thing monstrous and free. It was unearthly, and the men were—No, they were not inhuman. Well, you know, that was the worst of it—this suspicion of their not being inhuman. It would come slowly to one. They howled and leaped, and spun, and made horrid faces; but what thrilled you was just the thought of their humanity—like yours—the thought of your remote kinship with this wild and passionate uproar.

— *Joseph Conrad,* Heart of Darkness

Contents

Acknowledgments

The author wishes to acknowledge these fine publications where the following stories have appeared:

"A Different War" *The William and Mary Review*, 1999, Volume 37 (in a longer form)
"Caravan," *Monkeybicycle,* Volume 6
"Fever" *Pindeldyboz,* Summer 2007; and then *Taj Mahal Review,* Winter 2007
"In the Jukebox Light" *Dead Mule Review* and then in the anthology *Along the Lake*
"Marik the Rapist" *Greensboro Review,* Spring 2008
"Neighbors" *Smokelong Quarterly 18*
"Party Song" *North Dakota Quarterly,* Winter/Spring 2005
"Riverside" *South Dakota Review*, Winter 2001
"So this is Love" *Vestal Review*, Issue 27
"The Girl in the Halo" *Avery Anthology,* Number 1
"Think on Thy Sins" *Greensboro Review,* Spring 2007
"What about Meg?" *Antietam Review* Spring 1991 (named to the *1992 Best American Short Stories* Distinguished Stories List); also in *Love You to Pieces* an anthology from Beacon Press, Spring 2008
"Without Words" *And Now For a Story* (anthology) Casperian Books, 2008

"In the Jukebox Light," "Riverside," and "Neighbors" appeared in the chapbook, *In the Jukebox Light* from March Street Press (2004).

The Girl in the Halo

Some nights you swear the whole farmhouse will collapse around you. The phantom pain of approaching destiny shakes you from a near sleep, and the breathless, collapsing *whoosh* calls from the pit of your belly, and when you open your eyes, you expect to find yourself lost in a plaster-dust haze, surrounded by nothing but a network of rusty pipes and frayed wires. The roof leaks and the basement floods and the furnace's clanking song barely nudges the thermostat. Not a week passes where you don't find yourself replacing a fuse or chasing squirrels from the attic. And is it your imagination or can you actually hear the termites' wood-gnawing feast? The dull, unmodulating note cycles into your consciousness, possessing you, then slipping away, the *crunch, crunch, crunch* just another reminder of how powerless and consumed and infinitely small you really are.

You won't have money to buy sneakers until your next SSI check. "So you're going to fail your senior year because you won't take gym?" Coach Hill snapped after you'd sat out your third phys ed. class in a row. "What kind of knucklehead are you, Phillips?"

Your German pointer Daisy stinks like a laundry basket of wet towels. She's fourteen, a Methuselah in human years, and you can't remember life without her. "Not now, girl," you scold. Cereal bowl in hand, you nudge her side with your knee, trying to move her out of the way while you watch the morning news. With a sighing *harrumph,* she flops by your boots and drifts back to sleep. Raindrops tap the windows, and you think of the roof. The basement. The gutters.

And then, like magic, she appears on the screen. You've seen the video before—who hasn't?—the home movie full of reckless zooms and perspective-jerking pans. A newsman chatters in the background . . . *missing . . . leads in the case . . . the state gamelands closed for the day . . . search parties to scour the area* . . . and like the termites' munching, the voice disintegrates into a white blur. A lighted oval shines around one face, an editing room halo imposed to separate her from her frolicking girlfriend, and the halo, with its unblinking focus, says *Look. This is her.*

The girl wears blue shorts and a striped, sleeveless T-shirt. Her legs are firm (think of the hours she's practiced her backhand with her tennis instructor) and tan (so many afternoons spent lounging by the country club's shimmering pool). The background basks in a brilliant, unbothered sunshine that seems impossible this November morning. In the video, the girls wash a sleek red car, all the necessary props at hand, buckets and towels and oversized sponges. The girl in the halo flashes a toothpaste-commercial smile and raises a ringless hand to deflect the water spray from the other girl's hose. In her retreat, the girl in the halo kicks a bucket, and a white-bubble flood fans across the blacktop. The video slows . . . *look* . . . the water arching from the hose no longer a stream but a sun-reflecting parade of droplets and morphing globs . . . *look* . . . the girl runs toward the camera, and here, in a close-up of her bright, laughing face, the video freezes. *Here she is,* hisses the wordless transmission. *Look, look.*

Her name is Sally Hayes. For most of this Saturday's early risers, she's just another sorry victim, one more mystery in a life full of mysteries, and to these people, the thought of her drifts away, gone by the next commercial.

School buzzes with rumors. There are whispers of drugs. An

unwanted child. Nights spent in the arms of a black boy down by the river. And you know some are making up stories for the sick thrill of having the words leave their lips, for the chance to plant themselves in the perverted celebrity of Sally's disappearance. Blake Jennings—her on-again, off-again boyfriend—claims he was waiting at her house last Saturday night, but when she was late, he sped away, tires chirping, just another love-crazy kid in a hopped-up car, his night supposedly passed soothing his trademark temper with a pint of cherry vodka and a solo drive into the hills. Kristi Dickson swears on her backpack-lugged Bible that Blake, despite his history of keg-party fistfights and back-roads racing, was incapable of ever hurting Sally, but Daryl Stone claims he spotted Blake's red car on the other side of the Duke Street railroad crossing, and between the hopper cars' flickering, thundering parade, he saw a blond in the passenger seat . . . but when the caboose passed, the car was gone, the gate's zebra-striped arm raised over a deserted macadam patch. Everyone's got their hunches, but facts are in shorter supply. It's as if the truth, once so solid and known, has transformed into something slippery and gray and impossible to hold.

You take the roll of duct tape from behind the truck's seat and wrap the last, silvery strips around your boots' toes. Toss the cardboard roll in the rusted burning barrel and then smother it beneath the ripped tarp from the truck's bed. Of course the engine doesn't turn at first, your boot punishing the gas and the ignition grinding, grinding. You curse, hang your head, the stink of flooded gasoline a sentence to sit and stew for the next five minutes. Raindrops tear on the windshield, your view of your house and the cut acres of corn that once belonged to your family blurred by a dozen tiny streams. Over the past ten years, the land has been parceled off to your neighbors, a slow bleeding of pride and place until your house and barn feel like an island-speck adrift on a stranger's sea.

The truck starts with a backfire, and the nearby finches take to the sky. The wipers swat at the rain, streaked arcs that leave you squinting for a better view. Twice, the truck backfires on your rutted, stone lane. The heater doesn't work, and the AM radio around here is jammed with know-it-all talkers and Jesus freaks. Good Lord, the world would be a better place if people would just shut up once in a while. Ashen clouds stretch from horizon to horizon, a smothering blanket over the fields. The church in town is five miles away, and here you are, alone in your cold truck, another island in a world of islands, and you're thankful for the morning's silence because it lets you think about Sally, how she rode in your truck for the first and last time the day before her parents reported her missing. You and her and the others from your youth group had spent the afternoon chaperoning a casino night for the elementary kids—the day's gaming aspect protested by your mother alone—card tables and turtle races and games of chance where everyone was a winner and chips were cashed in for WWJD bracelets, inspirational CDs, and pocket-sized Bibles. Sally, the event's coordinator, had charged you with running the roulette table, and by day's end, you were dizzy with the ball's spinning dance and the shouts of over-stimulated children.

After the last parent had pulled away, you drove to the pizza parlor. Sally had asked because yours was the only vehicle which could accommodate everyone, but also, you suspect, because she and the others thought a ride in a shambling, rusted beast would be a lark, a type of redneck adventure. Still, you played along. Sally climbed in, her leg pressed against yours in the crowded cab, your arm apologetically brushing her shoulder as you shifted through the stubborn gears. In your dangling rearview, you watched the others in the back, their hair whipping in the breeze, their hands waving at Main Street's shoppers as if they were perched atop a homecoming float, and you took the corners gently, didn't run any yellow lights, your caution due in part to your concern for your riders but also to make the moment linger, to let yourself drown in the softness of her so close, the warm presence against your side making the distance between your reality and her life of horseback riding and mall shopping and SAT prep courses seem a bit less vast.

And the haloed video has now rippled across the country, an electronic echoing, her suburban whiteness and unthreatening beauty touching chords in strangers' hearts, for who hasn't known a girl like her? The once-tomboy who turned heads when she got glammed up for the prom, the girl who taught kindergarteners how to swim and who cheered the loudest at basketball games, the one who kicked off her sandals and turned spring-legged cartwheels across summer clover. In the video's twenty seconds, you and everyone else are free to channel her into the touchstone relationships of your life—sister, friend, daughter, lover.

A state trooper, his black hat sheathed in clear plastic, addresses you and the others. The bus hiccups and the trooper's hand clutches the silver pole behind the driver's seat, his beefy form swaying as he dispenses orders in a voice that reminds you of a puffed-up version of Coach Hill. Up front, a Boy Scout troop, slaves to authority and the power of uniforms, listens intently, as do the others—the church deacons and Sunday school teachers, the volunteer firemen, the boys from your youth group, even Blake and his father, who sit side-by-side in front of you. "You are about to enter a potential crime scene," the trooper barks. "If you come upon anything that looks suspicious . . ."

Lean your head against the cold window. The drops plunk the bus's sloped roof, and the rattle of turning shafts and axles invades your body. *Twelve . . . thirteen*, you count the yellow ribbons tied to Main Street's light poles, the posters bearing Sally's smile behind the rain-streaked shop windows, *fourteen . . . fifteen*. She's gone, yes, but not . . . The mystery left in her wake straddling this world and the next, leaving you all behind, a thousand Lilliputians tugging on your lines of hope, trying to pull her back, back.

"Something stinks," Blake's father says. Blake nods and glances back at you. Daisy's wet-toweled funk rises from your coat, and your hands clutch the hat in your lap, your fingers white with swallowed rage, your eyes cast down upon your duct-taped boots. When you were young, your mother said God had a way of evening the scales of life's injustices, but any adult not blinded by Jesus knows that's bullshit, and what more proof do you need than Blake's boy-band handsomeness and linebacker physique, his future assured not through hard work or good deeds, but through birth's dumb luck, his father the tri-county's largest developer, his fortune made on farm foreclosures and non-union wages and half-acre lots.

The last clumped houses of town drift by. And then the developments, new homes as big as your barn set on winding streets, stone entrance markers linking each neighborhood with the wildlife it's chased away—Fox Hollow and Deer Run and Quail Hill—the gold mines of Blake's inheritance, his family's money machine poised to gobble up the dormant, muted landscape of surrounding pastures and stripped orchards. Close your eyes and wish it all away.

And you don't resurface until the bus slows and you behold the tangle-wood snarls of the state gamelands. The packed-dirt trailheads bustle with activity, police cruisers and busses like yours, deputies on horseback leading single-file groups into the swallowing trees. Eavesdropping, you hear Blake's father say the police are acting on a tip, one of Sally's earrings sent in a letter with a scribbled note. Blake lowers his head, and his father turns and stares out the window. The rain falls harder.

The kerosene heater's light-headed stink greets you in the kitchen. Your boots squeak over the yellowed tile. An odd moonglow ebbs from the living room. Your mother sits on the couch, her shoulders wrapped in an afghan. A gospel station plays on the grease-splattered kitchen radio, another song about mercy and sin. Candles of various sizes and styles burn on the coffee and end tables. Dying buds of white-blue rise from the fireplace log.

"Mom?"

Daisy, her snout resting on your mother's slippered feet, raises her head. Your mother's eyelids flutter. "Didn't hear you come in, son."

"Is everything OK?"

She sits up, shuts the worn-covered Bible resting on her lap. "Fuse went out, just the living room. Didn't want to change it with the water on the floor. The candles look pretty, don't they?"

The place could go up in a second, your dreams of destruction come true, your shuffling dog knocking over an end table, and then . . .

"Shouldn't sleep while you're burning candles, Mom."

"You must be hungry. We'll have pancakes. And home fries."

"Great," you say, but how many days have passed since you last ate meat? Throw another log on the fire, some kindling. Sit on the fireplace ledge and take off your boots, your wet socks. Rub your toes, the skin red and numb, rows of wooden appendages that don't feel connected to your body.

"That man from the Navy called again. He's very nice."

"I'll call him later, Mom," but you know you won't. Years ago, you abandoned the notion of going to college, the thousands in tuition absurd when set against the backdrop of your life. Now the military, once your second-string savior, is fading with each passing month, the idea of your mother alone in the house, burning candles and changing fuses, too much to bear. She's not really crazy—is she?—rather, she simply doesn't care about much. You imagine her at casino night's roulette wheel, her measly pile of chips all bet on heaven, the wheel of fate spinning and the ball bone-clattering over the ridges, her eyes mesmerized by unwavering faith.

"I've been listening to the radio," she says.

"We didn't find anything. No one did."

She pats the couch cushion beside her. "Come pray with me."

You do as she asks. Daisy licks your bare feet, the rough-tongue tickle barely registering. "I was thinking about her voice," your mother says. "She had a beautiful voice. That solo she sang last Easter."

She clutches your hands. A rosy-pale nexus of nicks and cuts mars her fingers, a seamstress's scars, and her years of toiling over the dress factory's sewing tables have hunched her shoulders, ruined her eyes. Daisy sniffs your entwined hands. "Lord," she says, her eyes shut and her believer's smile lifting the corners of her mouth, "please hear our prayers for Sally . . ."

. . . and your thoughts rise from your body, drifting back over the last six hours, the gameland's muddy trails, the flared nostrils and breathy jets snorted by the sheriff's black stallion, the brush's fallen branches and decomposing logs, the rustle and thrash of your line's methodical march, the squirrels bounding through the ferns. A line of raindrops formed on your cap's bill, a ring of watery pearls that sloshed with each step, the drops gaining weight and falling one at a time. Trapped beneath the trees, parcels of mist rose from the forest floor, and it was here, in these hazy columns traced by falling leaves, that you beheld the staticky vision, the halo shining dully around her face, and hadn't the minister at your father's funeral told you the dead, released from the world's pain, belonged to everybody and everything? And there she was, an apparition you stumbled toward on unfeeling feet, breaking your line's rank until the sheriff blew his whistle. . . .

"Amen," your mother says.

"Amen."

You're late. Last night you sat for hours on the packed-dirt floor of Mr. Gittlen's foaling shed, you and the old man waiting on one of his mares. The foal emerged in lurching increments, its coat wet and shiny beneath the shed's naked bulbs. You and Mr. Gittlen dragged the foal to its exhausted mother and let her lick the slime from its eyes and nose and mouth. You didn't get home until after midnight, your sleep stubborn after the adrenaline of birth, and by 4:15 you were out the door, your truck rumbling down the empty roads on your way to your morning job at Zeager's dairy. You can sleep in study hall, you tell yourself, maybe Mr. Jordan's class if he shows another movie.

Three sweeps of the student lot and not a space in sight, and on each go-round, you pass Blake leaning against his red car, windows down and the stereo pumping, two wheels on the grass, he and his surrounding posse taking the last, stealthy hits off their morning joint, and after eighteen years of free passes and shortcuts, you guess there's no reason he and his friends should think the rules apply to them now. Up the long aisles you go, an orbiting, lost planet waiting for a taillight flash, a parent dropping off a lunch or forgotten report, and when a space finally appears, you take it. Books in hand, you jog down the long rows of parked cars. Time was this was a farmers' school, flannel and denim and blue FFA jackets, the earthy stink of cowshit on a boy's shoes no cause for scorn. Now the lot's jammed with birthday toys like Blake's car, with the sensible, late-model imports inherited from parents, cars that have toted their new drivers to hundreds of soccer practices and dance rehearsals, the back windows bearing the proud, faded decals of universities attended by older brothers and sisters.

Another day of charcoal clouds, the sun a fading memory, and winter looming. You step inside amid the last-minute locker slamming, the dissolving congregations of kissing couples and test crammers, and you shake your head at the way some have used Sally's disappearance as an opportunity to accessorize, yellow hair ribbons for the girls and yellow armbands for the boys, buttons, T-shirts with her smiling yearbook picture and a single word below: **Believe**.

The first period bell rings as you enter chem lab, the only class you had with Sally. The periodic table, with its array of families and groups and immutable truths, hangs beside the flag. "Let's settle in, people," Mr. Fink says. You angle your stool, a habit adopted to better study Sally during Mr. Fink's lectures, your perspective today drawn to an empty chair, and how many bleary mornings had you spied on her, her purple pen scribbling notes and Mr. Fink droning on as he held one of his molecules, a slapped-together collection of spheres and connecting sticks that reminded you of a child's toy. Earlier in the year, Mr. Fink had said that to understand an atom's proportions, you should imagine yourself standing in your backyard and the nearest electrons would be floating with the vapor-trailing jet planes. And this morning, you're thinking perhaps that's where the dead go, a man's last worldly gasp exhaled into every subatomic atmosphere at once. Poof.

Gone is Mr. Fink's mad scientist shtick, his Igor voice and his beaker tongs shoved up his sleeve, the clamps *snap-snapping* at the hall passes and papers handed to him. You slide on your safety goggles, the edges of your world warped, the plastic pressing its raccoon-eyes pattern into your skin. Up front stands a model of Mr. Fink Sally made one lab period from the molecule spheres and sticks, a seven-inch frame draped by a doll's white coat.

In a weary monotone, the real Mr. Fink speaks of breakage fees and proper cleanup, the risks of handling the nitric acid samples at each lab station. But his delivery is cut short by the eruption of yelps and gasps in the lab's rear. You don't see who's tossed the penny into the nitric acid, but it's impossible to miss the brown gas spewing from the beaker, the smell so pungent that the retreating students, their hands clenched over their mouths, knock over stools and notebooks in their retreat, and you're the only one who heeds Mr. Fink's muffled plea to open the windows. Gagging, your eyes watering, you struggle with the latch and fling open the window, your face pressed to the screen as you gulp in lungfuls of icy air.

You have the afternoon off, the neighboring farms gearing down for their winter's hibernation, provisions stocked and machinery stored. An hour, maybe two, until sundown, and you walk the treeline ridge that once belonged to your family, the field beside you left to fallow, its grasses scraggly and autumn-brown. From the treeline comes the moldy leaf smell, and nearer, the metallic scent of gun oil from the shotgun slung over your shoulder. From the ridge's highest point, you survey the distant activity, the ant-sized backhoes and bulldozers of Blake's father's company carving another niche out of the countryside. The machines' faint tremors ride into your boots.

"Come on, girl," you call to Daisy. The dog lumbers behind you, a hobbling stride that sets her ears swaying. Last summer, you walked her to this very spot with the intention of putting her down, the golf ball-sized tumor in her belly shown to you on an X-ray in the vet's office. Gnat swarms pecked at the wetness in your eyes, and the sun shone in piercing splinters through the ridge's leafed oaks. Daisy flopped down, panting, not looking back as you held the trembling barrel inches from her head.

But when the moment came to pull the trigger, your hands turned to stone and your head whirled with thoughts of years ago, how Daisy had moped for months after your father died, baying at the back door, whimpering soulfully as she prowled the barn each morning before curling up in his pickup's bed. You lowered the gun and led her back home. Four months later and you're still paying off the operation, and Daisy will be lucky to see spring.

The dog struggles to your side, and for her sake, you sit, and when she throws herself onto the dirt, a pair of mourning doves light from a bare oak. They're too quick for you to get off a shot, so you sit back and admire their flight, the synchronized splat of their wings, their gift of belonging to both the earth and sky. When you started hunting, you'd work this treeline with your father and Daisy, flushing rabbits and does, and in those silent moments before you squeezed the trigger, your father whispering advice behind you and Daisy frozen in her pointer's stance, you felt like part of something larger than yourself, perfectly in tune with the world beyond your skin.

In the distance, the bulldozers are shutting down, the gray sky quickly falling toward black. Time was you could sit here and not see another soul, the sky yours alone, the fields' leafy rows shimmering in time with the wind . . . and nothing stays the same, not your house or these rolling fields, not the people in your life . . . but if you shut your eyes and focus on the quiet, then perhaps a sense of that other time will find you . . . and you sit, still as can be, absorbing yourself in the textures embedded below your usual level of perception, Daisy's panting, the rustle of fallen leaves, the in-and-out mechanics of your lungs and the buried *thump-thump* of your heart. . . .

And the calm leads you back to your truck and the lonely drive back to the church to retrieve your forgotten coat, your mother's rectory key—its cutting earned through her unflagging involvement in rummage sales and prayer circles, spaghetti dinners and Christmas plays and choir practices—tucked into your jeans pocket . . . and over and over, you listened to the rattle of the water bottle Sally had left behind, a plastic tube that rolled from beneath the seat with every stop. Her car sat alone in the lot, and when you pulled alongside, she sprang out, smiling, the breeze billowing in her windbreaker's hood and the spitting rain causing her pretty eyes to squint. Her car wouldn't start, her parents away for the day, and Blake . . . well, she didn't want to talk about Blake . . . and would you be able to give her a ride home? Please?

Daisy lifts her head, a brainstem spark that calls through the years, and pulls herself up. You follow her, both of you moving forward on deliberate, hushed steps, and when she points, a three-legged stance on arthritic legs, you raise your gun and rest your cheek against the cold stock. "Go, girl," you whisper. Daisy lunges forward, stops short. The tall grass wavers, and a spooked ringneck shoots into the air. Beautiful, the bird's ascent, its wings spread in air-gobbling flaps, and your gun goes off, a swallowing, eyeblink explosion and a sharp kick to your shoulder. A spray of brown feathers flutters down, the shot echoing, echoing, then dying, the last hint of gunpowder carried away on the breeze.

The bird lies in the grass, a thoughtless impression. You slide a finger beneath the neck's white stripe and raise the limp head. Here and gone, you think. Here and gone. Daisy sniffs the bird's wing, then hobbles back toward home.

. . . .

Droplets trickle from your truck's opened gate, the bed hosed and swept clean. The finches flapping in the muddy puddle below scatter when your return with brown bags stuffed with envelopes and catalogues, cereal boxes and milk jugs. Empty the bags into the metal barrel, a paper and cardboard avalanche that blots out the soggy tarp. Lighter fluid hisses from the can's nozzle, and you shake and squeeze the tin a second and third time, a series of metallic sighs. The blue tip sparks against the barrel's rusted side, the match cupped in your hands for a protective moment and then dropped into the barrel. *Whoosh* sing the flames, the oxygen consumed in a breath-stealing rush, and you stand back, the sudden heat flushing your face, your boots shuffling until you plant yourself upwind. The scent is familiar at first, but then the tarp's plastic overpowers the rapidly burnt paper, the smoke turning black and acrid.

Open your truck's door and toss the cab's junk into the drum— gas receipts, a movie ticket stub, tissues and rags and snipped bits of twine. Wedged beneath the passenger's seat, you discover Sally's water bottle. Unscrew the cap and bring the opened end to your nose. Inside, the last swallows have hardened into ice.

A sheriff's cruiser trundles down the farm's narrow lane. On the porch, Daisy rises on feeble legs, barks weakly, and settles back on the sagging boards. The fire crackles, and short-lived sparks strain toward the clouds. The sheriff—a baritone in the church choir, an ex-teammate of your father's from their high school football days—parks behind your truck. You exchange greetings, small talk about the early chill, hunting, questions about how your mother's doing these days. The wind shifts, and the barrel's smoke momentarily wafts between you. He asks about casino night, if you saw Sally and Blake fighting, if she seemed upset, was she crying, did she say anything out of the ordinary.

"No. She was just herself. Happy the way she always was," you say. Toss the water bottle into the drum. The bottle rolls against the drum's side, and its plastic skin dissolves in the flames.

. . . .

A crystalline sky shines down on you, a taste of cloudless winter, the sun as brilliant as Sally's car-washing video. Gone are summer's living greens, the insects' mating chorus. Each breath freezes in a white cloud before your eyes. In the distance waits your destination and point of reference in this sea of tan grass, the row of leafless creek bank trees whose branches bristle against the blue sky. A second Saturday in the gamelands, you and the Boy Scouts, the deacons and the volunteer firemen, the guys from your youth group and Blake and his father comprising one of many squads scouring this wilderness. You cross the undulating field, your line's brush-tromping call just another chord in the symphony of barking bloodhounds, the two-stroke whine of nub-wheeled ATVs, the *thump, thump, thump* of a circling helicopter.

The dead are with us always, and you taste her on the sharp breeze, the her of everything and everywhere swallowed in each breath, the memory of her secure, bound and chained and unaffected by time, her solo's rising and falling notes on a sunshiny Easter morning. And you remember the cab-captured echo of her voice as the two of you neared her house and saw Blake waiting outside, arms folded as he leaned against his red car. Sally crouched down, her cheek touching your hip, her moist hand resting on yours as she implored you to keep driving. . . .

Suddenly, the hill-ringed vista narrows to a single copse of sycamores. A hound bolts ahead to join his howling mates, his leash hissing through the grass. The four-wheelers converge from your left and right, the sheriffs' stallions in galloping pursuit, and above, the helicopter's dragonfly dance, its blades kicking up frigid, dirt-swirling drafts. Blake and his father sprint across the rolling field, and soon, you're all running.

You catch your breath atop the creek bank's slope. A dog handler struggles up the bank, his yelping, protesting hound in tow. Below, the water flows, a shallow, gurgling march over smooth stones. On the muddy flat along the water's edge, men gather in a solemn circle. "No one else comes down unless I say," the sheriff commands, and you step back as a deputy laces a length of wind-bobbing, yellow tape through the trees and bushes.

Men come and go, and through the shifting activity, you catch glimpses of the naked body, the blue-moonlight skin and bloated flesh, her prettiness stripped away and scattered to the heavens. The helicopter veers toward the horizon, and curious birds return to the sycamores' branches. Blake, shouting and cursing, wrestles with his father and a deputy in an attempt to climb down the embankment, a struggle that dislodges the deputy's hat and rips the sleeve of his father's coat. Finally, Blake collapses, his fists pounding the dirt. In the field behind you, the Boy Scouts and the youth group teens kneel around one of the deacons, their heads bowed, many of them crying. The dogs sit obediently by their fur-stroking handlers and munch the snacks offered in reward for a job well done.

Alone, you consider the scene, the chaos and the closure, the simultaneous snap of a hundred Lilliputian ropes. You mother says all men are equal in the next life . . . and who knows if she's right or not, but in the currency of sorrow, all are equal in the here and now, and every heart must pay its allotted share.

In the Jukebox Light

At first we envied Tom and Betty's dancing. Friday nights at The Big Club, Saturdays at Mickey's, and none of us can remember a time we saw them in the arms of another partner. Crowded around the bar, we caught our breath and ordered the drafts that never quite quenched our thirsts, but Tom and Betty kept dancing, jitterbugs and twists, the new steps they whipped up on the spot that were as sharp as any on Bandstand. We dabbed our sweating brows with cocktail napkins and grinned discretely at the picture they made. Betty had left for college a pigeon-toed girl, and when she returned four years later, she brought home a teaching degree and an adult beauty that made us uncomfortable for not knowing the old her. The elementary school in town hired her, and at recess, the other men teachers, Principal Stevens included, fumbled and fawned for her attention, but Betty always opted to join her children, and her lanky frame ensured she was the first pick in the boys' basketball games, the one the other children ran to when a kindergartner needed rescuing from atop the jungle gym. A good six inches shorter, Tom had been the second-string center for our high school football team, our heavyweight wrestler's battered practice partner, and in the ensuing years, Tom filled out even more, growing to resemble the square butcher's block he worked over in McKalb's grocery. No one knew the particulars of their first date, but we were always happy to bump into them on the street because the sight of their intertwined hands—his thick nails tinted pink from years of butcher's blood, her fingers as slender as daffodil stalks—made us momentarily forget ourselves and believe, if only for a heartbeat, that perhaps anything was possible. On the dance floor, Betty's flat soles whispered and clicked, the hems of her sewing machine dresses ruffling, while Tom, moving with an odd, lumbering grace that surprised us all, answered with his asthmatic's wheeze and the pocket jangle of the loose change he never got around to spending on beer. At their wedding we rushed forward to take snapshots of their first dance, and in our returned photos, they float like blissful astronaut lovers in a sky of flashbulb stars. That whole next year they glowed the way just-marrieds do, the absent brushing of a misplaced curl, the distracted glances when the other took too long at the bathroom. When Betty's stomach grew and her thin ankles swelled, she and Tom abandoned their fast dances for slow tunes where they held each other with an intentness and devotion that blinded them to our inebriated ruckus, the crash of mugs dropped from clumsy fingers, the last-call fistfights that had the rest of us clambering onto our seats for a better view. Oblivious, their forms lit by the jukebox's blue-green glow, they circled each other in endless, delicate orbits.

Their boy lived for a month, and Tom and Betty haven't been to Mickey's since. Now we watch them the way any small town watches its sad stories, with concern and curiosity, politely distant as we sift for the telling details, but none of us has noticed more fat on Tom's T-bone cuts and Betty still teaches long division the way she did before. On our way home from the bar we've been known to park outside their house. We kill our engines and listen for the music from their windows. On tiptoes, we sneak across their lawn and tuck ourselves in among the bushes, and when the wind blows the curtains, we peek inside. They dance the way they once did in the jukebox light, slow and close, their new carpet worn in the tiny plot beneath their feet, the front of their clothes rubbed threadbare. Understanding sorrow, they have become like the rest of us. Or not. Either way, we can't stop looking.

Think on Thy Sins

T he branch snapped, a single, dry note distinct from the chainsaw's roar. *Snap*, and my daydreaming gaze abandoned the toddler in the neighboring lawn, his plastic mower spewing clouds of soapy bubbles. *Snap*, and I gazed up into Mrs. Hart's cherry tree, a mangle of half-dead limbs that would be lucky to see another spring. Twenty feet above me, my father's sun-backed form began a Plinko-ball plummet through branches both rotten and blooming. His revving, twig-severing chainsaw followed in his wake, and in the split second before they hit the ground, I thought not of the unforgiving, root-ribbed earth, not of his imminent pain nor his fragile bones, not what his injuries would mean to my half-finished semester at community college. I thought this—that here was one of life's rarest moments, a moment in which something of meaning was actually happening.

My father struck the earth with a thud and bounced like a sickly, under-inflated basketball. The chainsaw carved a thirteen-inch gash into his thigh and cartwheeled into a shade bed of hostas and ferns. Blood flowed, and his right arm lay bent in a series of so many angles that it barely seemed to belong to his body. Dislodged petals funneled down upon him, his jeans and hair speckled with a pink rain.

I dropped the branches I'd been carrying and sprinted to his side. Before he slipped into a twenty-hour coma, my father mumbled a single sentence. A breeze-swept bubble popped on his cheek. "The envelope . . ." he gasped between trembling lips, "the envelope is under the seat."

My father emerged from his coma like a diver surfacing from deep, frigid water, shuddering and gasping, his green eyes welling with a helpless panic. "The keys," he whispered, the words like dust motes rising from his throat. His uncasted hand groped the bed sheets until I dangled the jingling mass before his nose. I buzzed the nurse.

"Where's your mother?" he asked. Wincing, he glanced upward at the metal halo circling his head, his broken arm suspended by a system of pulleys.

My mother had been dead for over a year, and the rush of doctors and nurses saved me from breaking the news to him all over again. Tubes were checked, stethoscopes wielded. A doctor elbowed me aside and, pulling apart one of my father's lids, shone a pen light into his eye. My father's pupil constricted to a pinprick.

"Have you seen Sevak?" my father asked.

"I've been here since you fell."

The doctor checked his other eye. "How long has it been?" my father asked.

"A day."

He began to struggle, perhaps only then realizing his torso had been entombed in plaster. "Take what I asked you and go to the Mirage. Now."

The Mirage Diner. I'd always assumed its name was a mistake of translation, the fine-tuned nuances of English lost in this neighborhood which in the past decade had become known as Little Leningrad. I was still wearing my blood-stained jeans, and in my head beat the wings of a thousand hummingbirds, a threading drone of fatigue and hunger and too much caffeine, and dreamlike, the truck's low rumble through that spring Sunday afternoon, the terrain familiar yet skewed by the drifting scents of smoked meats and Slavic shouts, the pale children who played soccer in the street.

The sidewalks teemed with stout women in babushkas and old men who anchored themselves at folding tables playing cards and chess until long after sundown. In their former lives they had been murderers and thieves, shopkeepers and whores and doctors and bureaucrats and teachers and engineers, their lots traded in for a chance to redefine themselves on the far side of the globe.

I parked in the tiny lot behind the Mirage, observing a respectful distance between my truck and a tint-windowed Mercedes 500. I transferred the chainsaw and toolboxes from the bed into the cab. In any other lot in this neighborhood, my valuables would have disappeared in a heartbeat, my window smashed the moment I turned the corner, but this was Sevak's place of business, and even the pipeheads knew not to mess with that.

A bell rang, my entrance announced, and a palpable hush settled over the window-side booths and the opposing swivel stools along the chrome-bordered counter, my sense of unbelonging exaggerated by my stubble and bleary eyes and my murderer's clothes. The others resumed their conversations, flotsam nuggets of English in a sea of guttural Russian. I claimed a counter stool. I had tucked my father's large, brown envelope beneath my shirt, and its hard corners jabbed my torso. I ordered coffee, a cheese babka, and when the waitress returned, I told her I was Steve Jarrett's son and I was here to see Sevak.

I'd started working with my father when I turned fifteen, weekends and summer breaks, the leaf-falling October afternoons where he'd pick me up after school while my friends boarded buses or headed to football practice. "Tell me something you learned today," he'd say, and being the math-minded kid I was, I'd usually describe a parabola I'd graphed or a quadratic I'd factored, maybe a physics problem whose answer had lain at the end of a daisy chain of linked equations. "Smart boy," my father would say, and true, book work came easily to me, but one thing I wasn't so quick to pick up on was the logic behind my father's frequent abandonments of his mower or rake to talk to our clients. Or our clients' neighbors. Or just folks walking their dogs or pushing baby strollers. I wrote off his disappearances into mudrooms and garages to an entrepreneur's schmoozing, assumed the jottings he made in the little spiral notepad he tucked in his shirt pocket were simply reminders for an absent-minded man. Clues were all around—but I didn't put the pieces together until an August night outside the Mirage as I waited in the truck once again at the end of a long day while my father knocked on the kitchen door. Hours had passed since the time we'd promised my mother we'd be home, the days' previous rains forcing us to play catch-up with our lawns. A single, moth-swarmed light shone down upon him and the envelope in his hand, his moonlike body half-light, half-dark. The hair-netted cook who let him in scanned the lot, and when his cold gaze fell upon me, I finally understood my father's visits to the Mirage went beyond the string-wrapped boxes of smetannik and vereniki he always brought back to the truck.

"Come," the waitress said.

She led me through the kitchen's swinging doors. The heat of ovens and steaming dishwashers flushed my cheeks. The space bustled with the busy, cramped footwork of men in aprons, no doubt Little Leningrad's latest arrivals.

"Here," the waitress said. She was pretty in that angular Russian way, high cheekbones and coal-black hair, a wiry, athletic build that let me know she could probably smoke me in a hundred-yard dash. "He's waiting."

The air conditioner hummed in a room that was a dark sea of wood paneling. In the choked sunlight a computer screen glowed atop a paper-strewn desk, a light echoed by a muted portable TV in another corner. White ribbons shimmied from a humming paper shredder.

"Kyle, my boy," Sevak said, turning off the shredder. I'd always stayed in the truck when my father made his drop-offs, and I was surprised he knew my name. A framed photo behind his desk caught my eye—a much younger version of Sevak in a wrestler's singlet, his body braced for attack, his hands held out as if he were ready to spring forward and strangle the photographer. The Sevak now approaching me with opened arms was much thicker than the young man in the photo, his eyebrows bushier and his steel-wool hair twined with gray. His wrestler's near-nakedness had been replaced by a bright Hawaiian shirt, his wrist shackled by a platinum Rolex and his sausage fingers adorned with a series of squared-off rings. Yet, with his cool brown eyes and the smiling turn of his lips, he was still the same. In this neighborhood of shed pasts, it was whispered that Sevak was ex-KGB.

He embraced me in a spine-cracking hug and slapped my back with a meaty palm. He smelled like my grandfather's car, like cigars and cologne. Over his shoulder, I spotted his son Mikhail. Mikhail was engrossed in a copy of *People*, and the light of the TV shone on the glossy pages and on the dome of his shaved head. His T-shirt clung to his body, a fit that revealed not only a rippling mass of muscles but also a sleek .45 shoved into his waistband.

"We heard about your papa." Sevak stepped back, his hands gripping my shoulders. "He is going to live, right?"

"Yes."

"But he will be in hospital for long stay?"

"A month. Six weeks. No one's really sure."

"I will see him soon. You tell me what he needs and I will bring it. Your mama, she is gone, no?" I nodded. "I will have cook make you a pot of what you like. You pick anything off menu and Mikhail will bring it over. The mutton perhaps." He addressed his son in Russian. Mikhail nodded dutifully and turned another page in his magazine.

I handed Sevak the envelope. "My father asked me to bring this to you."

"Good, good." He angled his frame into the leather-squeaking chair behind his desk and motioned for me to take the seat opposite him. He slid open the bottom drawer and retrieved a bottle of vodka and two shot glasses. "So what is there for you now to do with your papa so sick?"

My answer was more of a reflex than a result of reflection. "I'll take over until he's better."

"But your school. Your papa is talking always about your school. He is very proud."

Since my mother's death, my father had adopted her dream of seeing me graduate from college. Perhaps it was his way of preserving a bit of her, something more meaningful than the blouses and dresses that remained in the back of his closet. "I'll manage."

Sevak poured the vodka and handed me a glass. His ring-heavy pinkie jutted out as he hoisted his glass for me to clink. "To your papa's health." He threw back his shot and sucked his next breath through clenched teeth, grinning. "Family, it is important, yes?"

I nodded, my eyes watering. The alcohol rocketed into my overtaxed brain, and for a moment, I lost touch with our conversation, my suddenly unmoored eyes drifting between the beefy forms of Sevak and his son. I wondered how many casts and comas and fractured skulls the two of them were responsible for.

"I will see your papa soon." Sevak stood, and I followed suit. He shook his head. "A shame though for me, too. Some neighborhoods where he works, the one with the gate and the trees." His hand waved like a magician trying to conjure a pigeon from thin air. "Oak Hill."

"Oak Knoll," I said.

"Oak Knoll." He patted the envelope. "I will miss Oak Knoll."

My attention drifted to the vodka bottle, its label written in a warped alphabet as indecipherable as a robin's song. How tired I was. I could have curled up on the floor and slept for a day, and for the second time, I answered in reflex. "I'm ready to take over all his business. That is if you want me to."

Sevak's deep brown eyes widened. He said something to his son in Russian. Mikhail smiled and turned another page. "This business is different than cutting grass. Big undertaking. Big responsibilities."

"I can do it."

"Do you know how to keep your papa's book?"

I shook my head.

"Sit," Sevak said. He poured two more rim-teasing shots and

slid his chair close. He peeled back the clasp on my father's envelope and dumped out his notebook and the rubber-banded block of bills. Sevak's thick fingers counted out ten twenties, a green wad which he stuffed in my shirt pocket. He opened the book and retrieved my father's little pencil and licked the tip. "Now pay attention, young Kyle. I'm going to show you something or two they don't teach you in college."

Business was my intended major—but when it came to my grades, business wasn't good. After my father's fall, I limped through the remaining weeks of the semester like a wounded animal, sponging notes from annoyed classmates, conjuring desperate deals with my professors to make up tests I'd missed. A week before finals I pulled up to the library, my mower-laden trailer commanding two spaces. My hands reeking of gasoline, my boots still flecked with grass and petals, I studied the library's burning beacons, the windows of surrounding buildings lit by night classes, a series of bright dioramas, each little bubble filled with the ambiguity of words, the artificial constraints of theory and conjecture.

The two months after the accident passed quickly. The day the hospital discharged my father, he squinted in the assault of mid-June sun, the pained expression of a bear emerging from his winter's sleep. Hindered by his monstrous brace, he used our toolbox as a stepping stool to ascend into the truck's cab. His eyes brimmed with a look like he was still falling, not panicked so much as coldly confused, his reliable footing gone, his prayers for rescue and security answered by the empty-aired grasping of his hands.

But for me, there was an unexpected happiness when I had my hands on the steering wheel of my father's truck, a brand of fulfillment no professors' words could define. And that happiness grew with each entry I jotted in my father's little notebook, with each envelope I placed in Sevak's ring-heavy paw. Money, I came to realize, was all around me, waiting to be had.

. . . .

By noon the Sullivan's backyard thermometer was pushing ninety and there wasn't a breeze to be had. Summer now, and no one scurried over the green world like landscapers or honeybees. I was half-jogging behind my forty-eight-inch Goodall, the throttle pegged beside the image of a hightailing rabbit, the mower's three purring blades gobbling up wide swatches of over-fertilized Kentucky bluegrass. I had six more lawns, and with the sun directly overhead, I was already worrying about twilight, my schedule delayed first by the usual hubbub at home (my father's boredom-driven nagging, his return to the truck still many weeks and therapy appointments away, his hobbling steps shadowing mine as he reminded me again that Mrs. Cates preferred pine mulch over hardwood and that Mr. Henson had complained about his flowerbeds' edges) and then by my stop at the Mirage (coffee to go and the latest line from Sevak, a hushed meeting with Mikhail in the back lot). At Oak Knoll's gated entrance, I was greeted with a horn-tooting scene of chaos, the booth's security guard refusing to raise the zebra-striped gate for a painter's van not on his morning list. On the other side of the gate, out rolled the Benzes and Beemers, the DVD-playing minivans with blond-haired children strapped in leather-soft seats, while on our side waited the incoming tide of this cultural osmosis, the plumbers and the maids, the dog groomers and personal trainers and electricians.

Inside the Knoll's perimeter of mature oaks and shadow-tucked security fencing, my timetable continued to deteriorate. After I'd trimmed his bordering row of sticker bushes, the recently widowed Mr. Shaw invited me into his sunroom and insisted I sip an iced tea as he explained the logic behind his Yankees-Angels teaser. Mr. Danielson simply pulled over and tooted his horn until I paid him curb service, a handful of folded fifties passed between us as he put a nickel on the Phillies weekend home stand. And the setbacks kept coming, most of them due to the opening of a previously untapped and very lucrative market for scrips of Xanax and Vicodin and Viagra, a whole pharmacy of human desires attended to by one of Little Leningrad's shadier doctors. This side venture had been hatched between Mikhail and myself, an enterprise we'd vowed to keep secret from Sevak. The Fosters' lawn was next, and as I double-stepped across the long stretch of their backyard, I was treated to dual visions. On one sweep, from behind the tinted privacy of my sunglasses, I studied Mrs. Foster and a friend on the tennis court's deep green surface. In their white skirts and gold bracelets, their headbands that matched their racket grips and ankle socks, they looked like two pieces of sugar-coated candy. And with a hard break squeeze and an about-face pivot, I'd set off in the other direction toward the chest-high chain link fence surrounding a lap pool, an undisturbed rectangle of sky-blue water. The Fosters' teenage daughter Claire lounged on a poolside chaise. Behind her sunglasses, I couldn't tell if she was asleep or watching me or reading the copy of *Vogue* opened in her lap. Sweat rolled down my back, stung my eyes, and I found myself wishing Claire would roust her newly curved body and take a dive just so I could hear the water splash and be reminded of how cool it would feel.

At the end of my next path, Mr. Foster stood waiting at the edge of his flagstone patio. He waved me over while studying the tennis court's lazy volley. I shut off the mower and took out my earplugs, bracing myself for some nitpicking complaint about the depth of his mulch or a growth of dandelions, their yellow heads striking a sense of injustice in his belly. My father said Mr. Foster had quite a rep as a divorce lawyer, a cross-examiner who could tear a prenup to shreds or make a sleep-around wife look like Mother Theresa. Last fall, Mr. Foster and my father had a falling out, an ugly exchange triggered by Mr. Foster's failure to comprehend a spread's half-point hook, his pride hurt more than his checkbook over the necessity of having his landscaper explain the nuances of a gambler's math.

"How are you, Kyle?" he asked. He wore his golf cleats, long white pants, and a yellow polo.

"Hot, Mr. Foster. Hot but good."

"And your father?"

"Out of the hospital. Getting some rest."

"That's good. He's fortunate to have you to take care of business." Small talk wasn't Mr. Foster's forte, and he fidgeted, his cleats scraping the patio stones. Obviously this conversation wasn't going to concern his lawn. I'd been getting used to this hedging with first timers, the search for words both understandable yet non-incriminating. "I'm looking for someone to help me with a delicate matter, Kyle. I hear you may be the man to see."

"Depends, Mr. Foster."

"I guarantee I'll make it worth your while." He glanced toward the pool. The undisturbed copy of *Vogue* rested on his daughter's lap. Was she sleeping . . . or studying us?

"Never know until you ask, Mr. Foster."

He took a deep breath. "I want someone hurt."

A summer twilight in Little Leningrad. The day's heat radiated off the macadam. A boy zipped past on a razor-wheeled scooter. The strains of Russian pop songs ebbed from the Mirage's kitchen windows, the staticky reception accompanied by Sevak's off-key baritone. My mower had been shut off for almost an hour, yet its hum lingered, my hearing still muffled from a day of earplugs and roaring engines, my sense of touch dulled by relentless vibrations. Mikhail leaned against his car's spoiler-topped trunk and sucked another drag from his cigarette. He grinned, the smoke trailing from an upturned corner of his mouth. "Tell me this story again," he said.

I repeated Mr. Foster's tale of the boy who'd stood up his daughter for her prom, highlighting the fact this wasn't a normal date but a coming out of sorts. Claire was a late bloomer, the kind of girl who'd been invisible until sometime during her senior year, and then, with a new haircut or more prominent bust, a less modest wardrobe or a saltier attitude, began to catch an eye or two. She knew the boy, who was a year older and was attending his first year at State, from their youth group and their high school ski club. Mrs. Foster had—in great secrecy—arranged the date, but Mr. Foster had believed there had been an actual spark between them, judging from the long, whispering phone calls they exchanged, Claire locked away in a room whose upper, dusty shelves still held her most beloved childhood dolls, the boy upstate in his dorm room, his spring break beginning the Friday before the prom. Mr. Foster said Claire, decked out in pearl earrings and a sleek black gown that had barely passed her mother's standards of decency, absolutely glowed. Claire's grandparents came with their new video camera, her aunts and uncles and a smattering of young cousins there as well to take pictures of the couple. The first giddy snapshots were taken on the flagstone patio . . . and for the next four hours, Mr. Foster was forced to watch that glow die in painful breaths, a heartbreaking descent documented in a dozen, sunlight-fading portraits. At ten, the boy finally called, half-drunk, from a gas station off I-95 in South Carolina, his plans to come home abandoned for a last-minute road trip bound for the Florida Keys.

"And that's it?" Mikhail asked. In the kitchen, Sevak berated his latest busboy victim.

"That's it."

"And he's rich?"

"He's rich."

"A thousand up front. Another when it's done."

We shook hands. "I'll let you know."

"Fucking America." Laughing, he flung his cigarette. "Nobody wants to get their hands dirty."

Mr. Foster glanced into the backyard and then motioned me into his garage. I set down my gas can and walked the driveway, past the sleek, red sports car that was Claire's graduation present. A blue and white tassel dangled from the rearview, a stuffed bear for the back window. The *thwack-thwack* of struck tennis balls echoed off the house's brick. The Fosters' maid, a sturdy Latina who moved with unhurried steps, dropped a bag into a trashcan and gave her employer a curt nod. Mr. Foster, standing just inside his two-car garage, waited until the maid shut the back door before addressing me.

"Did you talk to anyone?"

I treated myself to the garage's respite of shade. Another day in the nineties. Lawns all through my route were spotting brown. "I can arrange it."

He nibbled his lower lip. He seemed to be thinking, and I thought it polite to look away, my gaze taking in an oil stain on the concrete, a clump of cobwebbed tools, some paint cans with dented lids. "And?"

"Five thousand," I said, and I grew light-headed.

Mr. Foster's teeth released his nibbled, bloodless lip. "That's too much."

I shrugged. "The people who do this sort of thing aren't keen on haggling, Mr. Foster. It's more of a take-it-or-leave-it proposition."

He checked the incoming number on his ringing cell phone. "Let me get this," he said. "I have to pick up my wife. Maybe her flight's finally in." He paced to the other side of the garage, his agitated voice echoing.

I stepped back into the sun. On the Fosters' backyard court, Claire practiced her backhand with her tennis instructor, a spring-legged man with a nearly depleted basket of balls by his side. Claire swung and sent the yellow ball into the net where it fell and joined a host of others. "Better," her instructor said heartlessly. "Racket back, Claire. Swing through, nice and even." He demonstrated with a fluid display and then retrieved the basket's last ball. He struck it with a lazy grace, the ball bouncing in the same spot its predecessor had. Claire gathered herself with a bit of clumsy footwork and sent the ball sailing over the fence.

Mr. Foster joined me, a hand shielding his eyes. "I've got to go. Tell your friend he has a deal. Come by tomorrow. I'll have the money, and I'll tell you where to find this punk." He pocketed his phone. On the court, Claire helped her instructor pick up the balls. Each time she bent over, her pleated skirt rose, exposing a white-panty moon. "Three conditions though," Mr. Foster said. "One, this person knows nothing about my daughter or me."

"I think that's how he'd prefer it."

I followed him down the driveway. With a beeping button-push, his car lights winked and the locks slid up. He turned to me. "Two, I want to watch."

Witnessing. Here was Mr. Foster's bottom line. Still, I sought to dissuade him. "Don't think that's a wise idea, Mr. Foster. What if he recognizes you?"

"He won't. I've got it planned. No one will see us."

"He's not the type to carry a gun, is he?"

Mr. Foster snorted. "The kid played the flute in the marching band. He's a fucking anthropology major. What do you think?"

"And what's the third?"

"Hold on."

Claire turned the corner with her instructor. He carried the wire basket of balls, his rackets zipped up in a banjo-shaped bag slung over his shoulder. He was explaining once again the importance of mechanics, of practice and mental imagery. Claire's green eyes drifted toward her father and me. She offered a brief, conspiratorial smile as they strolled past. "You'll be hitting them back in no time," the instructor said, opening his car door.

Mr. Foster kissed his daughter's cheek. "I'm going to pick up your mother. We'll go out to dinner when I get back." Claire nodded and walked slowly back to the house. "Tomorrow then," Mr. Foster said. "We'll finish our talk, and I'll have your money."

I returned to my mower, but before I could pull the cord, Claire emerged from the house. She was still wearing her tennis skirt, her sleeveless top. She'd taken off her headband, and ringlets of sweat-teased curls framed her cheeks. Ice cubes rattled in her water glass. "You and my dad have had quite a lot to talk about recently."

"He's got a few jobs for me."

"That's cool." She licked water from her lips, dabbed her mouth with the towel draped over her shoulder. "So my friend Janice tells me you've gotten her scrips. That true?"

"Your friend Janice shouldn't spread rumors like that."

"Can you get Oxy?"

"It's not cheap."

She finished her water with a gulp and dumped the ice cubes on the lawn. "Come inside. I'll grab my purse."

Sunlight banners tumbled through the foyer's high windows, the afternoon's heat buried beneath the air conditioner's icy current. The checkerboard expanse of white and black tiles made me conscious of my dirt-crusted boots, so I stood on a tiny rectangle of carpet just inside the door. Claire crossed the foyer and disappeared into the living room. To my right stood a glass bookcase, each shelf arranged with crystal figurines, bears and penguins and horses whose insides shone with cold prisms.

Wallet in hand, Claire returned. "Forgot I needed to run to the bank machine."

"I'll be here for the next hour or two." I reached back for the doorknob.

Her hand grazed my side as she pushed the door shut. The soft pressure of her breast flattened against my arm. Her palm cradled my ass and then glided around to my zipper. "You take anything besides cash?"

Sevak sat across from me in one of the Mirage's window-side booths. A TV mounted high above the counter played a black-and-white western dubbed in Russian, a triple-digit station Sevak had wrangled from his cable box. The dinner crowd had left, only a few booths and a smattering of stools occupied. A cook and a handful of waitresses gathered by the TV, seemingly mesmerized by both the cadences of their mother tongue and by the resurrection of their old notions of America.

"Did your papa like the kournik?"

"Wonderful, thanks."

Since my father's accident, I hadn't left the Mirage empty-handed, the takeout containers of kasha and galushki and God-knows-what-else leaving greasy deposits on my passenger seat. After hearing how much our HMO was gouging us for my father's rehab, Sevak hooked us up with a woman who'd been an orthopedic surgeon in Minsk. We were happy to pay her a third of what the clinic wanted to charge; she was ecstatic to get out from behind the counter of Dunkin' Donuts and practice her trade. And Sevak's generosity went further, rippling out from the Mirage with every bill his thick fingers snapped from his pocketed roll, a twenty here for one of the soccer-playing street urchins to buy a new pair of sneakers, a couple hundred there to bail a son out of jail, envelopes stuffed every weekend for the neighborhood's christenings and weddings.

Sevak glanced over his shoulder. "Cowboys and Indians. I bet ninety percent Americans never seen one cowboy or Indian."

"Only on TV."

"TV, yes. In America everyone has TV to take away problems. It is your vodka, no?"

Sevak winked knowingly. He had taken a shine to me over the course of the past few months. Perhaps the assumption of my father's duties, both legal and not, appealed to his sense of loyalty. When I'd mentioned that I'd wrestled in high school (the only season that didn't interfere with a landscaper's duties), he cradled my jaw with his cigar-stinking mitts and kissed my cheeks, free now to reminisce with a kindred spirit who shared a past of self-starvation, of pain both inflicted and received.

"Look, Kyle." His pinky ring tapped the window glass. Outside, a woman crossed the street, her focus not on the traffic but on the scratch-off lottery ticket in her grip. She rubbed a nickel over the card, frowned, and let the ticket fall into the gutter. "Where there is money to be spent, there is money to be had. That woman, she has three dresses. One for Sunday and two others she switch back and forth. And still she buys lottery ticket. And they call me a criminal!" He laughed. "What a beautiful scam, Kyle. One dollar for chance to be rich. Who had this idea to sell hope for one dollar is a genius. A genius."

"Probably."

"I will tell you about capitalism in the way they don't teach you in school." He held an index finger at a forty-five degree angle. "Here is one line. Here is what it costs a business to bring you a something." Sevak used his other index finger to rise up and meet the first. His heavily hooded eyes crossed momentarily as he considered the point of intersection. "And here is what Mr. and Mrs. America will pay for that something. You know what this is called?"

"The break-even point."

Sevak smiled. "So you do pay attention in class. That is good. Break-even point, this is what most men live for, but not men like us." He winked. "And here, Kyle?" His hands drifted slowly apart, palms lifted toward the ceiling. "What is it above those lines?" He smiled at me. "Desire. That, my boy, is where the real money waits."

I nodded, listening with an intentness I never possessed in my classes . . . yet also distracted by the double-handed embrace that swallowed his coffee cup, the meaty fists that would pummel me into unconsciousness if he knew of my side-dealings, a beating administered not in the name of betrayal, but for the cold, economic fact that he hadn't received his cut. I found myself staring at those hands, the mountain-ridge knuckles, the wrinkles and scars, and when I could take no more, I turned and looked out to the sidewalk table where two old men stared down at a chessboard's unmoving pieces.

The announcing bell on the Mirage's door chimed, and a man I had crossed paths with in the Mirage's kitchen stepped inside. Sevak hugged him, tousled his hair, and took his offer of a folded sports page. I imagined the envelope tucked amidst the box scores, one more drop in the underground river that flowed through the Mirage, the tributes of pimps and dealers and bookies and loan sharks, the influx of powders and pills, illegal papers and forged documents, the human traffic of young men willing to sweat out seventy-hour weeks and the pretty young girls willing to do even more.

Rain began to fall, a few heavy drops at first, then a torrent, the Mirage's windows quickly blurring. I smiled, thinking of my thirsty, brown lawns. The lottery ticket bobbed away on a gutter stream, and a young man scampered past with a sopping cardboard scrap held over his head. The street's soccer players huddled beneath the grocer's awning. Raindrops drummed the diner's roof, and the cook turned up the TV. The dripping-wet old men who'd been playing chess migrated inside, their shoes squeaking, one grasping the board and moving with a pallbearer's metered steps, the other holding an umbrella over the trembling pieces. They claimed a booth near the register. Sevak joined them, and soon others had gathered around, nodding and whispering after each move.

On TV, the dubbed western reached its climax. On the dusty street of a lawless, untamed town, two men—one in a black hat, one in a white—faced off. Smoke plumed from their revolvers, and a still moment passed before the villain clutched his stomach and dropped to his knees.

Mikhail, his drenched shirt clinging to his muscled body, appeared through the swinging kitchen doors and cast himself into the seat his father had vacated. I slipped him the thin bundle of crisp hundreds under the table, our hands awkwardly brushing, and over coffee, I informed him of the job's details—the strip mall restaurant where the boy worked, his solitary, shift-ending trips to the dumpster out back. And then there was the matter of Mr. Foster's third request.

"This guy's kind of weird, Mikhail. He wants you to say something before you start on this kid."

"Like the little card that comes with the flowers. A greeting."

"I guess. It's from Shakespeare."

Mikhail took a napkin and patted the droplets rolling down the sides of his bald head. "I've heard of him."

"He wants you to say, 'Think on your sins.'"

"Think on *thy* sins. *Othello*, act five, scene two." Mikhail shrugged. "My father thought I should join the drama club in high school. He said it would be good for my English. Sometimes he forgets I was only two when we came here."

"Well, that's what he wants you to say."

"The Moor." Mikhail balled up the wet napkin and put it in the ashtray. "He says it before he smothers Desdemona. But the thing is Othello's all wrong. He's the one about to sin. Perhaps your friend should be better read. What else did he ask for?"

"He wants to watch."

Mikhail waved over the waitress. "You bring him and keep him out of the way. I'll make sure he gets a good show."

Under Mr. Foster's direction, I'd parked my mother's old compact car at the shadowed edge of the alley that ran behind the strip mall. Mr. Foster's watch beeped eleven. The other stores had closed, the front lot a macadam moonscape, the cars of the restaurant workers and the last indulging diners thoughtlessly spaced. A single streetlight burned at the alley's opposite end. A thunderstorm had passed within the hour, and an evaporating haze rose from the puddled blacktop. Inky clouds shrank from the moon. The store-side of the alley was a long row of windowless brick. Here and there, loading docks jutted out, the garage-like doors pulled tight and padlocked, the wooden skids stacked in rickety piles. A cat stepped from the scrub trees and gangly weeds that grew on the alley's opposite side. The cat performed a tightrope slink atop the curb, then scampered across the lot and disappeared into the shadows, a stretching, black space punctuated by the irregular pulse of Mikhail's cigarette.

Mr. Foster popped another piece of gum and tossed the wrapper out the window. He offered me a stick, and when I brought it to my mouth, I smelled his daughter on my fingers, my workday ending with me cutting the Fosters' lawn and dropping off Claire's scrip, her payment deferred for a naked romp in the downstairs powder room, Claire's skin still wet from the pool as she latched onto the window ledge and spied out on the slow, splashing progress of her mother's breaststroke laps. Mr. Foster chewed his gum with a crackling annoyance, a display periodically abandoned to hoist his binoculars to his eyes. In his khaki shorts, white sneakers and polo shirt, he could have stepped right off his backyard tennis court. He hadn't spoken since telling me where to park; so we sat there in the dark, waiting, once again, for one of those rare, terrible moments in life when something of meaning was about to happen.

Mr. Foster lowered his binoculars. "She didn't cry, you know. Not in front of us at least."

I guessed he was looking to somehow justify what was about to happen. I let him talk. Who was I to judge?

"She had problems. When she was born. It was touch-and-go for a week or two. The doctors didn't think she'd make it. I stayed with her the whole time, rubbing her hand, whispering to her, holding her when they'd let me. You don't know what that felt like, to have your baby in your arms yet not be able to hold her close because of all the tubes and wires . . ." His voice trailed off, a dry crumbling that stopped short of tears. "And in that hospital, I promised her that if she made it, I'd do everything I could to keep her safe. Everything I could to protect her. That's why I've worked so hard to give her the nicest home she could ask for, to send her to the best schools. And no matter how old she gets, I'll always think of her in my arms as I made those promises—"

The restaurant's backdoor opened. A soft flood of light spilled out around the doorway's featureless silhouette. Mr. Foster peered through his binoculars. "That's him."

I signaled Mikhail with a call to his cell, a single ring before I hung up. The boy—Mr. Foster had never told me his name, preferring to call him "kid" or, more commonly, "the punk"—placed a broom handle against the doorjamb to keep from being locked out. Lugging a plastic garbage can, the boy shuffled to the dumpster.

"Turn on your headlights," Mr. Foster ordered.

The boy froze, the dumpster lid half raised. Mr. Foster spit his gum out the window. Mikhail steamed from the shadows, balled fists held out from his sides, his neck flexing and stretching as if

he were joined together by a thousand tightly wound springs ready
to explode on this oblivious man-child whose only crime was
getting caught up in the heady moment of a college roadtrip, his
heartbroken date far from the innocent child her father believed
her to be.

Mikhail's mouth moved, Othello reborn in a skinhead's body.
Mr. Foster whispered the line, his mistaken *your* for *thy* that I
suddenly felt like correcting. Mikhail's first blow was a straight
right that caught the boy behind the ear. The dumpster lid
slammed, and the cat I'd watched earlier bolted back to the scrub
trees. The boy crumpled, his knees striking the ground. Mikhail
kicked the garbage can out of his way, a rolling canister spewing
potato peels, shrimp shells, and lettuce leaves. Mikhail yanked
the boy to his feet and unleashed a torrent of swift, torquing
body shots that doubled the boy over, a barrage topped off with
a roundhouse kick to the temple. The boy sprawled face-first
onto the macadam.

"Yes, yes," Mr. Foster said, grinning beneath his binoculars.

Scrambling on his hands and knees, the boy clawed his way
toward the restaurant. When he opened the door, the unleashed
tide of light shone on the perfect circles of Mr. Foster's binoculars'
lenses. Mikhail, giving unenthusiastic chase, delivered a kick to
the boy's backside. Assuming the fight was over, I started the car,
but before I could shift into reverse, the boy snatched the broom
he'd used to prop the door and turned on his attacker.

The handle cracked when it struck Mikhail's skull, a crisp, sharp
note distinctly related to the *snap* that sent my father tumbling
from Mrs. Hart's cherry tree. Mikhail and the boy stared at each
other, a showdown moment borrowed from the clichéd lexicon of
black-and-white Westerns, the boy clutching the broom's splintered
end, Mikhail patting the warm, sticky spill of blood dripping down
the sides of his domed head. Mr. Foster lowered his binoculars.

The boy's white shirt ripped when Mikhail yanked him back
into the alley. The sleeve tore at the shoulder, its whole length
coming free, a ghost limb snared in Mikhail's fist as the boy

stumbled toward the dumpster. Around and around the dumpster they went, the boy cowering, Mikhail brandishing the severed broom handle, a cat and mouse game until the boy ran toward us, perhaps mistaking our blinding headlights for some sort of salvation. Mikhail caught him ten yards in front of us, their drama unfolding on a floodlit stage. The boy fell, trying to cover himself as Mikhail swung the handle in a blurred bombardment that rained down upon the boy's head and shoulders.

"Think!" Mikhail snorted, punctuating each word with a bone-crunching blow, "Think . . . on . . . thy . . . sins!"

"Stop!" Mr. Foster said. He reached over and laid on the horn. The bleat reverberated off the brick's long expanse.

I shifted into reverse and floored the accelerator, my tires fishtailing over the wet macadam. The windshield scene dwindled but still remained in my headlight shine, Mikhail looming over the dazed and cowering boy, the broken handle raised, his blows more selective now, delivered with a cracking brutality to the boy's elbows and knees, the nubs of his spine.

I sped around the K-mart, past the gated garden section of sickly shrubs, the plastic-sack piles of tanbark and peat moss and composted manure. My front tire splashed into a pothole, my hubcap sent rolling across the lot.

Mr. Foster looked out the back window as we pulled out onto the street. "We can't let him kill him!"

"Shut up," I said evenly, "or I'll kick you out right here. It's a long fucking walk home, Mr. Foster."

Without exchanging another word, I drove toward the fast food lot where we'd met earlier. Humid currents drifted through our opened windows, the traffic sparse, the boulevard's long line of lights turning from red to green in a metered, domino-tumbling rhythm. We cruised past lit acres of car dealerships, past seedy bars with neon-burning windows and trendy clubs where sharply-dressed twenty-somethings posed hopefully on the other side of the velvet rope, past warehouse-big superstores and strip malls whose dimmed lights brandished corporate logos.

I pulled next to Mr. Foster's Beemer. "He's going to want more," I said. Mr. Foster was pale, his eyes wide and unblinking, and I knew the time was right to squeeze him for a little more.

"Our deal was—"

"Our deal was your boy was a flute-playing anthropology major."

Mr. Foster opened the door. The dome light cast stretching shadows over his incredulous face. "The price was set. You can't change it after the fact."

"You're not at the fucking Wal-Mart here, Mr. Foster. You saw the kind of person we're dealing with. Your flute player cracked his head open. He'll want more, and I'm not going to get my ass stuck in the middle. If you want, I'll give him your number and let you two work it out."

Mr. Foster climbed out and slammed the door shut. His binoculars swayed as he peered through the passenger window. "I'm not paying any more than another thousand."

"I'll see what I can do."

On the ride home, I thought of the boy, the ooze of blood between his fingers as he covered his face. I thought of Claire and the scent of sun-baked chlorine that rose from her naked skin. I pictured Mikhail in the Mirage's office, a vodka bottle in hand, his father grilling him as an émigré doctor stitched his wound. I imagined Mr. Foster driving beneath Oak Knoll's gated entrance, his moated sanctuary seemingly less secure than it had been just hours before, and I saw him pulling into his driveway, the welcome of a dark house and the blink of fireflies playfully floating above the dark expanse of his yard.

Soon enough, my father would return to the truck and take back his notebook. At the Mirage's counter, he'd proudly tell Sevak of my grades at State, a campus a few hours north where the snows came early and the heavy flakes plunged onto the ivy-covered halls. There, I learned about Smith and Keynes, Friedman and Galbraith and countless theories of cost and demand, poverty and affluence, risk and investment. What I heard little mention of was desire, that chaotic fuel of this sinners' world. But what reminder did I need of this fact beyond the nameless boy I'd sometimes catch sight of around campus, the one with the crooked nose and forehead scar, the boy whose wide, hesitant eyes reminded me of my father's after he was released from the hospital? Every time I saw the boy, I wanted to go to him, to explain in some way or another, wanted to confess and, perhaps, be forgiven, but what could I say? What in the world could I say?

Neighbors

H ear that?" asks my wife Amy. Books in hand, we relax on our patio. A shaft of late-day sun borrows through the maples' leafy canopy and deposits a dazzling, sunlit pool on Amy's lap.

I put down my book and listen to the faint threads of sound. A box fan rattles on our bedroom windowsill. A freight train chugs along the cornfields outside town. Squirrels leap between the maple branches, and the orioles snipe back with their cheep-twittering complaints. "Hear what?" I ask.

"Exactly." Amy grins and returns to her book.

What luxury, this tranquil evening, our neighbors, the Shertzers, guests of a wealthy uncle in Cape May, ten days of sand castles and boogie boarding and excursions on the uncle's twenty-foot sailboat. The Shertzers' Sunday morning departure was more circus troupe escape than suburban exodus, the pell-melling ruckus of their preschool twins and one toddler (the last child an eight-pound surprise, a little girl conceived against all precautions. "Must be something in the water," Paige Shertzer joked when she told Amy and me the news) corralled into a vehicle already bursting with suitcases and beach umbrellas, straw hats and folding chairs, snorkels, flippers, plastic buckets, and a dog-gnarled Frisbee. Amy and I stood curbside with the adult Shertzers, Tim in his Hawaiian shirt and white shorts, Paige in macadam-slapping flip-flops and a pair of sunglasses whose curved glass held our dark reflections. The minivan door slid shut, an action which stirred the beachy scent of sunscreen, the children's fair, freckled skin already lathered beneath double-digit SPF lotion. "Don't worry about your cat," we assured them as we exchanged hugs and handshakes. "Don't worry about your plants or aquarium fish, your mail or morning paper—we'll take care of it all." Hugh and Luke cried, "Let's GO!" in their eerie twin unison, the barrier of steel and glass unable to mute their shrill commands. We laughed, amused by the boys' impatience, their sailboat-dreaming anticipation. With a toot-toot, the van pulled from the curb, and Hugh and Luke strained against their protective strappings to wave their mirror-imaged good-byes.

Amy and I bookmark our pages and set out for our evening walk. Twilight, and the graying backdrop sharpens the lilies' orange blooms, the first blushing tomatoes in well-staked gardens. I capture a firefly and hold out my hand for Amy to admire my green-blinking prize.

We cut our route short because there's business to take care of back home, sex business. The red-circled fertile days are marked on our refrigerator calendar, the fluctuations in temperature and mucous flow duly noted in a logbook Amy keeps with the devotion of a ship captain's log. *Hurry, hurry,* say her quickened steps, perhaps the heavens have aligned themselves, perhaps tonight's the night— but her pace eases when we come upon a young couple pushing a stroller. Amy squeezes my hand, her eyes fixed on the carriage's doze-drooling passenger, her touch an emotional anchor against the blood-streaked memory of two miscarriages. The water that flows into the Shertzers' house doesn't reach ours, a fault of plumbing of one type or another, and nothing bruises my heart like the appearance of a tampon wrapper in the bathroom waste can.

We climb onto the Shertzers' porch. Nearly dark now, and the neighborhood cats haunt the shadows. Summer moths dance beneath the streetlamps, while down the block, a porch light flicks on, a beacon to a child late to return from his afternoon of play. My knees crack as I stoop to pick up the newspaper.

Hot inside the Shertzers' foyer, the still air flavored with the accumulated scents of other lives. Unfamiliar shampoos and soaps.

Traces of Christmas potpourri and fireplace ashes. Oiled baseball gloves and kitchen spices. A sense of stalled activity lingers in the mute spaces, the feeling of an amusement park after closing time. Balls of assorted shapes and colors peek from beneath the sofa and kitchen table. The twins' grass-stained sneakers lie in a mismatched heap by the back door. A dancing Snoopy adorns the only glass left on the kitchen counter.

Splitting up, we perform our neighborly duties. I fill the cat's dishes and sprinkle fish flakes over the aquarium's bubble-rippling surface. Amy nudges back the house plant leaves and pours water onto the parched dirt. I study our house through the window above their kitchen sink, briefly taken back by the skewed perspective, the darkened rooms, the ragged hedges I should cut. I fill the Snoopy glass from the tap, take a sip, and offer the glass to Amy. As she drinks, I playfully flick the water clinging to my fingers, and the droplets bead on her cheeks and throat.

"Come on," she urges, and with a T-shirt tug, she leads me upstairs. We take cursory peeks into Tim and Paige's bedroom, the boys' domain of cowboy-sheeted bunk beds, the brimming toy chest, and the hamper stuffed with soccer uniforms and mud-cuffed jeans. In the nursery, Amy cracks a window, and the breeze tempers the room's stifling warmth. Our shed clothes blanket the floor beside the crib, the two of us naked in this talc-scented world of tinkling mobiles and outlet covers. We settle our once-supple forms onto the carpet, and before mute witnesses of stuffed animals and half-dressed Barbies, we once again unfurl our hopes like canvas sails, waiting for a wind that may never blow but in which we must believe.

What About Meg?

rue weightlessness. Professor Steven Bridges achieved it last year, a sensation he would later describe to his worrying daughters as skating forward on warm blue ice, frictionless and unworldly beautiful. According to the attending emergency room physician, Steven Bridges was deceased at the time, but no matter. He is, he would honestly tell his younger daughter Claire, if she had the nerve to ask, looking forward to experiencing it again.

With its new set of plastic valves, Bridges's heart beats stronger than ever and that is fine with him, yet he can't help but think of it in odd ways. In the shower he often fingers the scar, smooth and raised from his skin, and envisions his heart as something no longer human, like an old steam boiler locked in a school basement, chugging away through the Pennsylvania winter.

There are other changes, subtle yet undeniable changes, he keeps to himself—Claire thinks he is unsettled enough as it is. He has acquired a taste for Scotch, a glass or two with water and ice now part of his nightly routine. As he sips, he stands on the balcony deck overlooking the backyard, swept up in a tide of smells he has never noticed before, smells of fragrant perfumes and gasoline and blooming honeysuckle. Below him, a neighborhood cat slinked across the painted key of Bridge's driveway basketball court. And then Bridges gazes upward to the stars, reciting the names of constellations he learned as a boy, wishing he could be sucked up into their vastness.

Tonight it is pleasant, the crisp air creeping down from the mountains and settling in the quiet valley streets. Bridges finishes his drink and steps inside to retrieve the cell phone Claire bought him for Christmas last year. It's late, but he can't sleep. Too many thoughts swim through his mind. The house is still, the stillness in turn magnifying the fall of his footsteps and the hypnotic *chunk-tha-chunk* of the ceiling fan. He pauses by the open door of his older daughter's room. Meg, thirty-eight and retarded, sleeps in her canopy bed, snoring unevenly through her gaping mouth. Bridges stops to consider her, stuffed toys bunched by her head, the blue moonlight that bathes her like an oversized angel, and he wonders what her dreams are like, if they are free and uninhibited or if they are dull, full of the syrupy thoughts that permeate the rest of her life.

"Claire?" Bridges says into the receiver. Phone in hand, he has stretched the length of his burly frame across the deck. The wood is cool on his neck. In his hand is the picture of Sarah he keeps in his wallet. She has been dead nearly three years to the day.

"Daddy?" Claire mumbles. "That you?"

"Claire, sweetheart, would you do me a favor?" His words drift as he studies the blinking lights of a passing plane.

"Daddy, are you OK? Do you want me to come over?"

"I'm fine, sweetheart. Just do me a favor and go to your window. The stars are beautiful tonight. I wouldn't want you to miss them."

"It's after midnight. Are you sure you're OK?"

"Humor your father, sweetheart, and go to the window."

Claire drags herself out of bed and looks to the sky. "They're beautiful," she says, unimpressed.

"Claire?"

"Yes?"

"I've decided to sell the house."

There's a moment of hesitation before she answers. "But, Daddy," she asks softly, "what about Meg?"

. . . .

Bridges leans on the banister and yells up the stairs, "Come on, Meg."

"OK."

"Don't want to be late again, do you?"

"I'm coming, I'm coming!"

A door slams. Footsteps scurry overhead. Bridges walks back to the kitchen. The smells of coffee and bacon filter through the house as he makes breakfast. Ever since Sarah's death, he's prepared Meg's meals and made sure she's gotten to work on time.

Meg flops into the kitchen. Awkward and pear-shaped, she carries herself with a choppy walk that borders on being totally out of control. Strands of wet hair are plastered to her cheeks, the rest pulled back in a sloppy ponytail. Her eyes are dull blue and bloodshot red, still circled with sleep lines. With a heavy grunt, she sits at the breakfast table and cradles her ample face between her hands.

"Every day it's the same thing," she says. "Get up and go to work. Come home, watch TV, go to sleep, and go to work again. It's boring!"

Bridges smiles weakly as he turns bacon slices in the skillet. For the last week everything has been "boring." In the past, there have been months full of "crazy," "fascinating," and "ridiculous" things.

"How many eggs do you want, dear?"

Upper lip raised, she scrunches her face in confused wrinkles. "Why eggs all the time? Eggs are so boring."

"So you don't want any?"

"I'll have two." She holds up two fingers and twists her hand back to front.

Bridges sits and sips his coffee as she eats. His head is light from last night's Scotch. He could smell the alcohol creep into his sweat as he completed his morning workout—one hundred push-ups, two hundred sit-ups—the same amount he did in his semipro hockey days. He is blessed with the muscular chest and thick arms of a man half his age.

He watches his daughter, her feet widely spaced and planted firmly on the ground, as she concentrates on not letting any food spill onto the red-and-white-print shirt and matching red skirt all the female employees at the Pancake House must wear. She has been working the three-to-eleven shift for thirteen years, longer than any other employee and over twice as long as her current manager. A wood and bronze plaque from the national office of Pancake House Inc. commemorating ten years of service hangs by the refrigerator.

"It's good," she says, looking up to him, her mouth full of food. The thin, powder-blue window curtains cast a watery light over her face and the exaggerated motions of her chewing. "Oh, I almost forgot." She waves her hands as if she has just burnt her fingers. "NBA's Greatest Games is on ESPN 2 today. Don't forget to tape it, OK?"

"Sure," Bridges says. Women's, men's, games old and current, biographies of famous players—Meg will watch anything dealing with basketball. On Tuesdays, her day off, she sometimes sits mesmerized for hours watching her tapes. Her thoughts, so forgetful and ragged in terms of everyday duties, swim with hoop stats—rebound leaders and field goal percentages and three-point sharpshooters. Before Bridges corrals her into the car, she sneaks in ten minutes on the driveway court, graceless layups and two-handed set shots, palm-slapping dribbles that have her hunched over in concentration, the ball often careening off her foot and ending up in Bridges's flower garden.

Meg stares out the window as they drive. Sunlight flickers between the roadside trees, the glare so bright off the hood it nearly shuts Bridges's eyes. He checks his watch and decides to take a shortcut through campus.

"Look, Daddy!" she says. She points with a series of piston thrusts. "It's the stadium!" Lips drawn tight in concentration, she counts silently on her hand. "Only two months to football!"

The stadium rises from a lush summer field, all cement and exposed steel girders and strangely hollow in the July haze. Bridges used to take his daughters to a few games each season. Claire lost interest after junior high, but Meg and Bridges have gone to every home game for the past fifteen years (season tickets—a faculty perk). Dressed in blue and white like a slice of autumn sky, she raises her fists and screams, stomping boldly on the aluminum flooring, holding onto the cheers for a second or two longer than anyone else in their section. And at the start of the second half, when the students sing their version of the alma mater—a repetitive, in-tune chant of "We don't know the goddamn words!"—she covers her mouth with her mittened hands and glances sideways at her father, her blue eyes streaming with tears as she attempts to restrain her laughter.

"The net's broken," she says. "Can you fix it?"

"It's just one of the loops at the top, honey. It's OK."

"But when it's broken the ball doesn't fall right." Her smile wilts. "I like it to fall straight down when it goes in."

"OK, let me look into it." Bridges pulls alongside the curb beneath the slanted red roof of the Pancake House. "Pick you up at eleven, dear," he says. "Have a good day at work."

"You always say that." She rolls her eyes. "It's so boring to hear that all the time. Now don't forget about the basketball show." She slams the door and scurries toward the entrance, nearly bowling over a mother and her stroller.

"Meg!" Bridges calls out, but she has already gone inside. On the seat of the car is a red apron and a red name tag. *Hello,* the tag reads, *My name is MEG.*

Hercules. Lyra. Scorpius. Bridges reclines on the wooden planks of the balcony deck and traces the patched quilt of the sky with his sausage-thick fingers. A six-inch reflector telescope gathers dust in the basement. It is a monstrous thing, undeniably expensive, a birthday present from Claire. He has used it before, to pinpoint comets and photograph lunar eclipses, but for the most part he leaves it alone. The power to focus obliterates the relations between worlds. It is better, he thinks, to view the heavens unbroken to truly appreciate their splendor.

Air conditioners drone through the humid night, and Bridges detects the odor of fresh mulch from a neighbor's garden. A loosely gripped glass of Scotch rests on his scarred chest. The ice cubes swirl with each breath.

He raises his hand and touches the stars. Canis Major. Leo. Hercules.

The cell phone sits on his stomach, but he has turned the ringer off. He is tired of it. Claire and her thousand well-intentioned but exhausting questions. Meeting dates set with realtors. Confirmation calls to the directors of local and state agencies for retarded citizens. He lifts his head, takes another sip, and glances toward the house. Meg's window shines with the pale glow of her Spiderman night-light.

He rises and leans against the railing, surveying the patch of macadam beneath the basketball hoop. Three years ago, Bridges took a pipe cutter and chopped down the backboard's pole, although he can't actually remember doing it. He thinks of the sailors who first crossed the ocean and the astronauts who sat on the launch pad, waiting to be hurled into space. Nothing, he thinks, is certain until it is part of the past. He upturns his glass and lets the ice cubes tumble to the earth. The cubes clatter like wind chimes in the wet air.

In the kitchen he pours another drink. Ice is piled to the rim, and it numbs his lips. He takes a seat at the kitchen table. Being alone at night does not bother him. There is an embracing coolness to the indigo light, to the shadows of familiar objects. In the three years since Sarah's death, he has made a practice of avoiding his home until evening. Claire invites him over for dinner at least three times a week, and Bridges knows he stays later than he should. He spoils his grandsons with presents and does push-ups with them riding his back. Claire worries about the stress this puts on his heart, but she knows it would do no good to argue with him. She just smiles and sighs, a throw-your-hands-up, *What am I going to do with you?* sigh.

It is only during the day that being alone in the house becomes difficult. Bridges can't stand the way the late afternoon sun slants in through the windows and lights up the place like an unused museum. Tables and vases wade in puddles of white sunshine—all the things Sarah and Claire bought over the years—they might as well belong to strangers. Bridges secretly fears that the soft areas of his heart have been roped off.

He retrieves the spiral notebook he hides in the cabinet above the refrigerator. Inside the notebook is a list he is making, a list of everything he owns. He has decided that when he moves, he will get rid of it all. Claire and Meg can have whatever they want and the rest can go to charity or the dump. Making the list swells his heart with joy. It is like seeing his house new for the first time, each room whitewashed and vacant. He picks up a pen and walks into the living room, and with each page he completes, he is engulfed by a warm, buoyant wave, a wave that carries him so high he must duck his head from hitting the blades of the slowly turning ceiling fan.

Bridges balances atop a rickety stepladder, hooking a new net to the hoop's rim. There were thunderstorms last night, but today it is beautiful, and he squints against the sun's piercing brilliance. His ladder-exaggerated shadow stretches beyond the top of the painted key. He is bare-chested, clad only in khaki work pants and his paint-splattered work boots. Sweat gleams beneath the tufts of gray hair on his forearms.

He gazes down upon the court, remembering the humid summer day he sprinted to this spot to find Sarah, who Meg had hounded into playing yet another game of HORSE, lying in a heap. Like a grainy nickelodeon short, the scene still plays ceaselessly in his mind—Meg withdrawing to the lawn, where she sat silent and stunned, her basketball resting on her lap, her fingers anchored in her mouth, Bridges attempting mouth to mouth on a pair of lips that had already turned the color of sick moonlight. The emergency room doctor said Sarah had suffered a massive coronary infarction, that she was most likely dead before she hit the ground. Meg was treated for shock and didn't speak a word for the next two weeks.

And Bridges, drunk for only the second time in his life, took it upon himself to hack down the backboard's pole the night of her funeral. Dressed in his somber blue suit, he fell asleep on a lawn chair to the lullaby of crickets, his fingers coated with the pole's rust flakes, the backboard resting beside him like felled forest tree. When Meg finally broke her silence, her first request was when she could play basketball again. Within a week, Bridges had repaired the pole, feeling foolish for his drunken escapade.

"Daddy!"

Bridges looks down and sees Claire gazing up, a hand shielding her eyes. She is out of breath, her hand resting on the curve of her seven-months-pregnant belly.

"Hello, sweetheart."

"I looked all over the house for you." She draws a deep breath. She does not say, "I was afraid I'd find you sprawled half naked and nearly dead on the kitchen floor, the way I did last year," although he can tell this is what she's thinking.

"You know your sister. She doesn't like her net tattered."

"I don't like seeing you on a ladder," she says. Her tone is alternately relieved and concerned.

"Haven't you heard?" He taps his chest. "I have modern medicine on my side."

"Honestly, Daddy," she sighs.

The afternoon sun lights her brown hair. Suddenly, Bridges is taken back by the tiny scraps of his wife that rise to the surface of his daughter's face. He secures the net's last rung and slowly climbs down. "Let the games begin."

"She at work?"

"Until eleven." At the foot of the ladder, he gives her a hug. The baby inside her responds with a kick.

"So," Claire says, pausing for a second before continuing, "you're really going to sell the house." She hugs herself as if caught in a fall breeze. "You know it won't seem right driving by and not being able to stop in."

He folds up the ladder, allowing her to take the top end as they walk it back to the garage. He wishes he could tell her about the list in the spiral notebook. Wishes he could summon the words to explain how, even at this moment with nothing but blue sky above him, he can feel the entire weight of the house—the kitchen tiles, the plumbing, the plaster, everything—pressing down upon him.

"So what are you going to do?" she asks.

"I've been checking into apartments and condos in town. The whole thing is up in the air right now. Maybe I'll travel for a while. I've got three semesters of unused sabbatical."

"What about Meg, Daddy?" Her words echo in the garage's shadowed space.

"I've been making some calls; it's all stuff we've discussed before, sweetheart. Remember last year when we put her name on the county's list for group home assignments?" He looks to her and waits until she nods in agreement. "They called and said there's a placement open for her."

Claire bites her lip. "She won't like it," she says quietly.

"I know." He takes the ladder from her grip and secures it to the hooks bolted into the wall. "It was easier when your mother was alive. Now it seems I spend half my life dragging her out of bed and driving her to work, patrolling the house to make sure she hasn't left the iron on or the bathwater running. I don't think I can do it anymore." He smiles and winks at her. "And she can't come live with you, can she?"

Claire bows her head, trying to conceal her own smile. Just the week before, Meg and Bridges had joined Claire and her family for Fourth of July fireworks down by the lake, and Meg, with her hands clasped over her ears, howled with cries of joy that had scared the wits out of Claire's two sons.

"When are you going to tell her, Daddy?"

Bridges studies backboard and pole, a still life perfectly framed by the garage's doorway. "Soon," he says. "It'll have to be soon."

"Claire's house!" Meg exclaims. Bridges nods as he drives Meg home from work. The night is dry and cool. Meg waves at Claire's house, a brick two story, even though the windows are dark and there is no one in the yard.

At home, Bridges tries to watch the final ten minutes of a DVD he's rented. He has not seen a movie in a theater since Sarah's death. Meg has a tendency to call out to the characters on the screen, to laugh out loud at all the wrong times. Ripples of whispers and giggles flow through the theater.

Bridges sits on the couch. "I'm going to watch the end of my movie," he explains. Meg takes off her apron and plunks herself down on the opposite end of the couch. "I've only got a few minutes left, then you can watch whatever you want."

"What about the basketball show?" she asks. "You did remember to tape it, didn't you?"

"Yes," Bridges says. "We'll watch it after this, OK?"

Bridges starts the movie. A love scene plays, two shadowy figures drawing closer. The actress kneels on a mattress, the room clouded with misty blue light, and allows her shirt to slip off her shoulders.

"Oh, Daddy!" Meg screams. The long Indian earrings Claire bought for her in Mexico flap against her neck. She laughs hysterically and covers her eyes. "This is so BORING!"

Bridges stops the DVD. Without a word, he leaves the room and walks to the deck. Meg follows. All day long—in the shower, in the car, as he mowed the lawn—Bridges has rehearsed the speech he plans to give her. He puts his arm around her shoulders and breathes deeply. The night is full of cricket calls and the scent of honeysuckle, and he wonders if this is how he will always remember this moment.

Meg gazes down to the driveway. "Can I shoot a few now before the show?"

"It's too late, honey," he says. "Dribbling would wake up the neighbors."

He studies her in the soft light that spills from the house and notices with sudden astonishment that she is middle-aged. Her temples are wrinkled and bordered with gray.

She moves away from him. "I want to go in and watch the show, OK?"

Bridges nods and lets his opportunity slip away.

The show is about game five of the 1976 NBA finals, a triple-overtime epic between the Celtics and the Suns. Bridges watches along with his daughter, struck by the dated fashions of the players and fans, by the indoor haze of the sweltering Boston Garden, by the younger ghosts of men now old. And at a deeper level, he is awed by the game's back and forth miracles, by its desperation and pathos, by the unlikely heroes who came off the bench to turn the tide after the stars had fouled out.

Bridges turns to say something to Meg, but she is already stretched out and snoring on the couch.

It is after midnight, and Bridges sits on the deck. The sky is bruised with strips of deep blue clouds. Soon it will be autumn. Soon the Saturday football games, the roar of 70,000 foaming over the town. Soon Cygnus, Pegasus, Auriga, and Orion. A full moon steps silver over quiet houses and manicured gardens. A romance of chirping insects rises from the maples, an electric buzz like the tingle of Scotch.

Three weeks have passed, warm summer days and twilight evenings of HORSE and twenty-one, their driveway transformed into a scene of overtime drama where Bridges has repeatedly counted down a game's last seconds as Meg, her face set in steely determination, heaved a game's last shot, the clock and scenario reset with each miss until she sank the winning score.

Bridges gazes over the driveway court and contemplates tomorrow's deadlines. The realtor wants to start placing ads in the local papers. The director of the group home insists on a definite answer or else Meg will lose her placement. Bridges takes another sip and sighs.

He freezes at the sound of the garage door sliding halfway up. Fearing burglars, Bridges draws away from the railing, stares, and slowly shakes his head. She takes the court in her shorts and laced-up hightops. The ball never abandons her hands as she pantomimes dribbles and shots, her feet leaving the ground in clumsy, two-inch leaps. She bounds along, cheered on by a crowd only she can hear, an imagined world Bridges will never know but to which he feels a tremendous and tender allegiance.

Riverside

Distant streetlights touched the chrome of the cars in the funeral home lot. Hot again tonight, humid, the crickets restless. Moths hurled themselves at the naked bulb above the parlor's back door. Mary let herself inside and tiptoed unnoticed downstairs. For the past year, she'd been moonlighting at Sager's Funeral Home, a connection made after her fiancé Ted had died in a water company ditch collapse. Hushed organ music came from upstairs, the carpet brush of shuffling shoes, the familiar sounds of an evening viewing. Mary opened her black suede bag, and the harsh overhead light reflected along the length of her scissors. A man in his mid-twenties, naked save the swaddling white sheet covering his midsection, waited on Mr. Sager's metal table. Mary had read about the accident in the Sunday paper, a kayaker sucked into the lowhead dam, the trapping currents that spun him like a washing machine rag. Mary had worked for Mr. Sager long enough to know drownings had their own unique coloring, a faint bluish tint that survived embalming, making them appear colder than the others. She began to cut his hair, and dirty blond strands, full of the natural waves her salon customers dreamed of, fell upon her open-toed sandals. Young ones like him still bothered her, the hunting accidents, kids pulled from drunken car wrecks, the ones who'd choked on fate or their own ill tempers. With their smooth skin and hair unbothered by age or chemo, they seemed like an entirely different species than the withered corpses who usually occupied Mr. Sager's table. Mary stepped back and judged her work. The basement, with its high school chem lab stink, always made her a bit lightheaded, a sensation heightened by the high-pitched buzzing of the electric razor she ran over his stubble. *Wake up, little dreamer*, Mary thought as she brushed the cut hairs from his neck and face with a barber's soft brush. *Wake up, Snow White.* An immaculately pressed black suit and a pair of matching slacks hung on a nearby rack. On another hanger, a stiff-collared white shirt and blood-red tie. A pair of mirror-polished black shoes rested on a chair, and beside them, Mr. Sager's trademark, a white carnation for the suit's lapel.

A scratching at the basement window distracted Mary, and when she looked up, she gasped, dropping her makeup kit, momentarily frightened by the two kneeling boys staring down at her. The boys scattered, and the flowerbed dirt their sneakers kicked up pelted the window glass. She'd caught them before, fingertips and noses smudging the pane, their eyes wide with horror-show curiosity. Using the flat side of her pinkie, Mary spread a thin layer of blush over the young man's cheeks. Tonight's job wasn't as bad as she'd expected. No gashes, no visible bruises, no need for Mr. Sager's pink-beige mortician's putty, a hue that never quite matched natural skin tone. Next, a smear of lipstick, a powderpuff dabbing over his brow. Her potions lit his face, and his moonshine radiance softened. Funny, how in this room where customers never complained, she often felt a deeper responsibility than she did in her own salon. A muffled sobbing called from above, a ripple of consoling voices. Mary blended her coloring along his throat. No denying he was handsome, high cheekbones and a sleek swimmer's build, rope-muscled arms. At her salon, radio songs and gossip occupied Mary's mind, but in the relative hush of Mr. Sager's basement, her thoughts couldn't escape the silent faces she worked upon. Reaching out, she allowed her fingertips to graze the kayaker's cool lips and wondered if he'd suffered greatly, if he'd tried to call out a loved one's name, soundless bubbles that broke the river's surface with the flavor of his breath and the fading rhythm of his heart.

The morning of the kayaker's funeral, Mary drove along the river road. Powerlines from the nuclear plant ran above her, snaking shadows on the road and the hood of her car. At first she missed the dirt road turnoff Ted had shown her, and her wheels spun on the gravel shoulder as she backed up. Her shocks moaning, she bounced down the rutted, sloping road. Scraggly weeds and low, hanging branches scraped against her car. She parked in a grassy clearing along the water's edge. The salon didn't open until eleven, a once-a-week treat to herself. Another sultry night had passed, and on the opposite bank, a grayish haze meshed with the hillside's green-leafed maples. Mary sat on a large boulder and let her eyes become unfocused by the river's sun-speckled flow. Yellow butterflies pestered the slender milkweed pods. Mosquito clouds hovered above the shoreline's muddy puddles. Mary untied her sneakers and stepped into the river. This had been Ted's secret fishing spot, a shallow ledge sheltered by an upstream bend. Easy to imagine him here, the spin and hiss of his cast line, his pants rolled up and the water lapping at his knees. Their ring of campfire stones remained on the shore, but now they were half buried in washed-up silt. The water soothed Mary's feet. The dark outlines of fish darted at her approach. She waded out, enjoying the sounds of her own splashing. The current pushed against her, and between it and the uneven bottom, she swayed slightly on her next step forward.

A trio of crows lit from a nearby oak, flapping wings as loud as Chinese firecrackers. Crouching, Mary let her hands slip into the water. She remained as still as a body on Mr. Sager's table, not even flinching when an electric blue dragonfly buzzed her head. She pictured Ted in the same pose, washing his hands, rinsing a gutted fish before tossing it in a skillet. She was thankful for such memories because they balanced the image of him in his casket, the forever dreamer's expression on his face and a white carnation in his lapel, but after her months of working in Mr. Sager's basement, even that memory didn't bother her as much as it once did. What haunted her now was the in-between time, the blackness of a collapsed ditch and the weight of choking earth, the thought of him so alone with his fear and pain.

In time, the perch returned, more than she'd ever seen. They slid by her shins, brushed against her hands. Mary's back ached from her stooped posture, yet she didn't move. A perch slowed, its spinning fins tickling her palms. Mary stared into the copper-colored water, studying the fish, her distorted hands, and wondered if she'd ever seen anything so beautiful.

With a sudden squeeze, she yanked the perch from the water. The other fish scattered, a velvety shimmering beneath the river surface. The perch squirmed, but Mary's fingers, strong from working her scissors, held the slippery body in place. The fish's gills rose and fell like frantic bellows, a slow drowning in the honeysuckled air. Sunshine flecks glistened in its black eyes. Mary waded back to shore and set her catch on the large gray boulder. The perch twisted and flipped, and the droplets that arced from its tail quickly evaporated on the warm rock. Mary rested her palm against the fish's cool scales, waiting for the heartbeat that separated the living from the dead.

Party Song

T im Atkinson sat in his parked car outside Dave and Paige
Killington's apartment. The Killingtons had spent the past
twenty months renovating the second floor above Paige's antique
shop, the walls that once divided the space into student apartments
knocked down, the floors stripped of beer-stained carpets and
refinished in woodsy hues, the space furnished with the chairs and
lamps and bookcases Paige had accrued from her flea market
prowlings. Tim blew into his cold hands. Two years before, he
and his then-wife Dana had huddled with the Killingtons and their
blueprint plans, and as they opened their third bottle of wine, Dana
made Paige promise she'd have a housewarming party when the
project was complete. A series of setbacks had timed the celebration
with Halloween, a coincidence that promised an even giddier
celebration.

The antique shop's plate glass windows stood dark, the displays
of Amish furniture and the rescued detritus of forgotten generations
nestled in the shadows. A costumed pack of students strolled past,
and their faint reflections momentarily swam in the murky glass.
An older couple splintered off from the students. The man, a horn-
wearing devil, rang the foyer door buzzer beside the antique shop.
Tim sat up a bit straighter, trying to determine whether the nurse
shivering beside the devil might be his ex-wife.

In Tim's lap rested his improvised costume, a ridiculous shag
wig and a string of oversized wooden beads. He slid the clanking

beads around his neck, then bent forward and fit the wig's elastic band over his scalp, the rearview mirror twisted as he tucked back the escaping strands of his own hair. Dave Killington, one of Tim's psychology department colleagues, had asked Tim if he was OK with Dana being invited to the party. "Of course," Tim had said, hoping his response's conviction would mask his apprehensions, especially now since Dana had started seeing another man. Tim gazed up to the apartment's slightly fogged windows. Another couple rang the foyer buzzer. Tim, his fingers resting on the door handle, felt like a hesitant child standing poolside, too afraid of the water's chill to leap in and join the others.

Tim's car bucked rudely, his heart seizing until he realized a young man had hopped onto his rear bumper. The white-robed Samurai leapt off, the car bouncing again, and rejoined his plastic-sword duel with Robin Hood. Oblivious to Tim, the two men battled down the street as their friends cheered.

Tim climbed from his car. Up in the Killingtons' apartment, a woman's silhouette stood before the living room's corner window. The dueling swordsmen disappeared around the corner, the street hushed in their wake. Tim crossed the street, rang the foyer buzzer, and completed his disguise by sliding on a pair of dollar-store sunglasses. Climbing the steep stairwell, he patted the wig's synthetic fibers, feeling simultaneously embarrassed by his admittedly lame costume, yet also protected by it, its covering providing the slimmest of barriers between himself and the world. The door at the top of the stairs opened and out stepped Dave Killington in the scuba gear he hadn't used since the vacation Tim and Dana had taken with the Killingtons four years before.

"Now the party can officially start," Dave said, squeezing Tim's shoulder as he guided him inside.

A chalk-faced man in a rippling, black cape approached the folding table in the room's far corner. His protruding plastic fangs nibbled his lips, and his deeply mascaraed eyes surveyed the table's array of alcohol and mixers.

"What kind of beer do you have?" he asked in an accent more Pennsylvania Dutch than Transylvanian.

Marooned behind the table, Sherri Witman rolled up a sleeve of her white shirt and fished through the icy water of the cooler at her feet. "We've got lagers and lights, but the stouts are going quick." She stood, and the ensuing blood rush pulsed against the knot of her black bow tie.

A ballerina appeared at Dracula's side. Her chiffon tutu nudged the tabletop's tip cup, a container which hadn't seen much action since Sherri's ante-starter of two ones and a few quarters. "Dracula should have a Bloody Mary, shouldn't he?" asked the ballerina.

"Very good." He snapped into character and bellowed: "Dracula will have a *very* Bloody Mary."

"Make it two," chirped the ballerina.

Sherri blended the concoction, creatively making-do with the limited supplies. Vodka splashed onto her fingers, and its flush of quickly evaporating heat and its bitter-clean scent chilled her. For nearly five years, she'd been sober, and even though she spent every Tuesday night at the local bar, she hadn't counted on the unsettling urges brought on by the repeated handling of alcohol. Her right eye twitched, tiny spasms of distress. She'd taken this job as a one-time favor to her cousin Amy, the owner of a fledgling catering business. Sherri handed over the Bloody Marys and then wiped her hands against her hips.

Partygoers in elaborate costumes crammed the living room. Dracula danced the mashed potato alongside an angel whose pipe-cleaner-and-aluminum-foil halo bobbed atop her head. Sherlock Holmes used his magnifying glass to study a framed etching. The ballerina's silky slippers whispered across the hardwood floor. Abraham Lincoln adjusted his phony beard. Overlapping voices echoed off the high ceiling, the wainscoted walls, and depression-era glass fixtures. A hint of marijuana smoke laced the air.

Sherri turned and gazed out the window at her back. The Killingtons lived above the old hardware store, now one of four antique shops along Main Street. Sherri sighed at her own bad luck of living in this town her whole life, yet missing out on the gentrification craze that had priced her out of her last apartment and was threatening to do the same with her current one. She rubbed her palm against her twitching eyelid, and with her other hand, she opened the window. Cool air rushed in, the raucous voices outside suddenly distinct. Clumps of costumed students maneuvered along the sidewalk, French maids and bikers and cape-sporting superheroes, and their voices—cursing, flirting, laughing—rose to Sherri. A plastic sword duel broke out on the street between a green-felt Robin Hood and a robed Samurai. Spurred on by the onlookers who raised their beer bottles in a Roman salute, the duelers battled around light poles and mailboxes and fire hydrants, the Samurai leaping on then off a parked car's bumper. Sabers rattling, Robin Hood—or was it Peter Pan?—and the Samurai battled down Main Street, and Sherri's attention turned to the just-pounced-upon car's exiting driver, a man who paused to adjust a ridiculous wig atop his head before crossing to her side of the street.

"How's it going?" asked her cousin Amy. She set down a silver hors d'oeuvres tray, poured herself a sliver of bourbon in a plastic cup, and downed the liquid in a shuddering gulp.

Sherri closed the window. "Perhaps I should be the one asking you."

"Is it obvious what a wreck I am?"

"Not yet, but the night's young." Sherri wet a napkin corner and dabbed the lipstick smear on Amy's upper lip. "Everything's fine. Don't stress."

"This is so important though." Amy gestured toward the crowded room. "Word of mouth with this bunch could be a real boost. College gigs, faculty functions, tea services for visiting deans. It would be a step up from catering fire hall weddings."

"I had my reception at the fire hall."

"And look how that turned out." Amy gripped the bourbon bottle's neck, then let go. "Who's looking after Jason tonight?"

"Your mom, believe it or not. She's probably teaching him seven-card stud."

A Daniel Boone in coonskin cap and fringed leather jacket ordered two beers, his money retrieved from the gunpowder horn slung over his shoulder. Dave Killington, wedged into an unflattering wetsuit, answered the doorbell and let in the man Sherri had watched getting out of his car. In half steps and pauses, the two of them became absorbed into the crowd, their places marked by the flyway tips of a shaggy wig and a bright yellow snorkel.

"Will you make a round?" Amy handed the silver tray to Sherri. She turned toward the kitchen and sniffed. "Is that smoke? I have to pull the crab puffs from the oven."

"I've never served before." Her reflection swam between the toothpick-speared morsels. "Bartending I know, but—"

"Just walk around. Be patient. Smile." On her way to the kitchen, Amy called over her shoulder: "I'll be two minutes."

The tray held tightly, sometimes raised above her head, Sherri waded into the crowd. She navigated pathways clogged by unwieldy outfits—a devil's curling tail, a football player's wide shoulder pads. The partygoers, their cheeks flushed with the room's budding warmth, continued their conversations as they picked across Sherri's tray, and she overheard talk of the troubles with the college's foreign exchange program, a proposed expansion of the football stadium, a new method to chemically date prehistoric artifacts. Outside of "What are these? And this one?" and "Thank you," no one spoke to Sherri, their costumed backs turned as they bit into their stuffed mushroom caps.

"Thanks, darling." Amy took the tray. "I've got it from here. There's a little line going at the bar."

"Who's first?" Sherri asked, sliding behind the table. She mixed a vodka and grapefruit for a tipsy reverend, a boilermaker for a pigtailed Dorothy. The line grew, and Sherri shifted into a higher gear, not bothering to notice costumes or the growing bouquet of green bills billowing from her tip cup. Daniel Boone had returned, and as Sherri opened another beer for him, he spoke to the ballerina about the paper he was writing on the nesting habits of the red-backed vole.

"Miss? Miss?" called the ballerina.

"Coming," Sherri said. A sweat broke across her shoulders as she hustled to meet their demands. The table that separated her from them was only a few feet wide, but tonight that distance might as well have been a mile, a chasm carved by the social hierarchies that separated server and guest, by their dissertations and sabbaticals, their tenure and long summer vacations and decent health benefits. On her side of the table all that waited was a lifetime of unrelenting labor, her mind-numbing bank job, the voice and piano lessons that claimed what little free time she had, the raising of a son who at the age of five was already showing disparaging glimpses of his father's wild side. And above all, there was the daily struggle to stay sober. The line dwindled to the last two, the scuba-geared host and the man in the shag wig and sunglasses.

Sherri sighed through her server's smile. "What can I get you, gentlemen?"

Dave Killington pushed aside his snorkel's mouthpiece. "A rum and coke for me and a beer for my hippie friend."

Sherri mixed the rum and coke while the scuba diver and the shag wig continued their interrupted argument.

"Our culture is horribly stagnant," Dave said. He raised his goggled mask and sipped his fizzing drink. "Ours is an age of regression and lowered standards."

"Aren't you being a tad overdramatic?" Tim asked.

"We live in a nation obsessed with celebrities and sports teams and criminals, the more perverted, the better. And God help us all if another O.J. comes along and mixes up all three. Doesn't that—"

"There you are, Tim!" called Dave's wife Paige. A circle of stiff, Elizabethan ruffles tickled her chin, and the rhinestones of her queen's crown glittered in the light. After a material-ruffling embrace, she tapped Tim's chest with the egg-shaped end of her scepter and reached into her gown to produce a pen and paper scrap. "I want you to jot down a unique and hidden talent, good sir. Anything that comes to mind."

Tim took the paper, thought for a moment, then scribbled a response.

"Splendid." Paige folded the paper. "I'll put this with the others."

Tim turned to Sherri. "I missed the whole back story on this. I'm not getting myself into anything weird, am I?"

Sherri grinned. "Guess that depends on what you wrote."

"If our society became flesh," Dave said, pausing to take another sip from his drink, "it would be receiving its last rites."

"I think it's impossible for a culture or society to become truly stagnant." Tim picked at his bottle's label. With the arrival of each new guest, his eyes drifted toward the apartment door. "One might not appreciate its changes, but it is changing nonetheless. You're just focusing on the negative. The segment of the population you're berating now has always existed. They were the same folks who cheered the lions at the Coliseum, and their like-minded descendants brought picnic lunches to public hangings. But there are other, more telling barometers of a society."

"Such as?" Dave asked. "Reality television? Talk radio? Pro wrestling?"

"How about the arts?" Tim sipped his beer. "The history of art, like all other histories, is the opposite of stagnation because it hinges on moments of departure, of risk."

Dave scoffed. "If that's true, what would today's great leap be?"

"Who knows? All I do know is that it's happening. Somewhere, someone is making that leap."

"Name one that's happened in our lifetime." Dave swirled ice in his cup. "Just one and I'll buy your argument."

Sherri, who couldn't help eavesdropping since the men hadn't abandoned their spot in front of her table, piped up, "What about when Dylan went electric? Or the first time Hendrix restrung his guitar."

Tim smiled. "That's two, Dave."

"Point taken." He set down his glass. "May I ask for a topper before I venture off . . . I'm sorry, what is your name?"

"Sherri." She pointed to the nametag on her blouse. "The pin doesn't lie."

"Sherri, you're doing a wonderful job. The queen and I are quite pleased." Dave studied her. "You look very familiar. I've been thinking so all night. You wouldn't by chance sing sometimes at that bar down the street?"

She splashed rum over the ice cubes in his glass. "Every Tuesday night."

"You're wonderful." Dave turned to Tim. "She really is. We've seen you a number of times." He rose onto his flippered toes. "Wait until I tell her majesty. She really is something else, Tim. She's a professional."

"I'm hardly a professional. Did a few years in Nashville. Studio work mostly. Some gigs. Not near enough to live on." She twisted off another beer top. "And now I'm back where I started from."

The music stopped abruptly. Battling her gown's flowing train, Paige climbed atop a kitchen chair and raised her scepter in a gesture of silence. "May I have the attention of all my pretty subjects? Is there anyone who hasn't submitted a written confession of a hitherto-hidden gift? No? Then let's proceed with tonight's main attraction, a talent, or lack-of-it, show."

The rustling and maneuvering of unwieldy outfits accompanied the exodus to the living room. Balanced atop her center-stage throne, the queen pulled a paper scrap from a mixing bowl. "Now who among us can recite from memory every vice-president in the history of your rebellious little colony?"

An occasional guest trickled back to Sherri's post, but for the most part, she was left alone. The crowd's mood grew more festive. Fits of laughter accompanied the sight of the registrar's ear wiggling; applause for a grad assistant's recital of *Romeo and Juliet*'s balcony scene. Dave's officemate executed a muscle-quivering handstand walk across the floorboards, and his drooping kilt triggered hoots as it revealed a pair of equally plaid boxers.

Tim worked his way around to the kitchen entrance, a positioning as close as possible to the mixing bowl. Strange, his green-tinted world, and thank goodness for the cover the lenses provided. He reasoned his paper was bound to be near the top, and he resolved to snatch his entry if the opportunity presented itself. His stomach knotted every time Paige reached into the bowl. In the room's cleared center, the notoriously stuffy assistant dean danced a shoe-whispering moonwalk. Tim's department head yanked up his shirt and turned his pale, hairy stomach rolls into a disturbingly hypnotic imitation of an ocean wave. Almost contagious, the crowd's merriment, its hoots and whistles mingling with the first hints of Tim's buzz. Perhaps he shouldn't be worrying at all, his confessed hidden talent requiring a prop he didn't think the Killingtons owned. But his budding euphoria was snuffed by the sight of Dana at the crowd's opposite end. How pretty she looked in her black jeans and black, skin-tight shirt, a pair of furry cat ears fixed atop her head and a long black tail switching from her back belt loop. By her side stood Paul Harding, a coworker from Dana's office, and from the rumors Tim had heard, Dana's new boyfriend. Dana's smiles and laughs wrinkled her painted-on whiskers. Tim slumped against the kitchen doorway, his head swooning.

Paige drew another slip of paper. "And who," she asked in a regal voice, "can play 'Classical Gas' on the guitar?"

Tim cringed. He hadn't picked up a guitar in years.

"I know Tim can play," called a voice from across the room.

"Is this true, Timothy?" Queen Paige asked.

Dana studied him and offered a peacemaker's wave and a semi-embarrassed shrug for she, more than anyone, understood his wallflower's discomfort. Tim cleared his throat. "I'm not claiming to be a virtuoso—"

"Then we demand a performance."

Tim's heart jerked. "That would require a guitar and—"

"I believe there is a guitar in the kingdom." She turned to her husband, her haughty tone momentarily abandoned. "Isn't there, honey?"

Dave twisted his snorkel from his mouth. "I believe so, dear. In the boys' bedroom. Might need some tuning."

"I'm terribly rusty," Tim said. "I don't think—"

"We shall grant you ten minutes of practice before the concert begins. If you would, darling."

Dave's flippers slapped the floor as he led Tim from the living room and down the narrow hallway lined with closed doors. "The boys are at my mother's for the weekend," he explained, opening a door covered with ill-proportioned drawings of pirates and cowboys and mysterious beasts. "Hope you're having a good time," Dave said. He closed the door behind him, and the alcohol on his breath flavored the darkness. After a bit of fumbling, he flipped the switch, and Tim discovered himself planted in a chaotic, miniaturized world. Coat piles smothered the beds, allowing only jigsaw peeks of blankets patterned with astronauts and rocket ships. Dave knelt at the entrance of the boys' toy-spilling closet. T-shirts and building blocks and plastic airplanes flew over his shoulder until he unearthed a long-necked, pear-shaped black case.

"Bought it for Mark last Christmas." Dave opened the lid. "Doesn't get much use anymore. Which may be a good thing if he inherited my musical abilities." He handed the guitar and a pick to Tim. "I'll be back in a few."

Dave closed the door on his way out, and the barrier muffled the party's ruckus. The guitar balanced over his knee, Tim plucked the strings and turned pegs until the sour notes mellowed. He strummed a few chords. The strings' vibrations resonated into his hands. In his thoughts, he constructed the first bars of "Classical Gas," his fingers straining to recall what had once been so familiar. A riotous gale buffeted the shut door, and in the uproar, he detected the distinct sound of Dana's laughter. Tim took off his sunglasses and rubbed his watery eyes. He lined up the first chord, but when he tried to start again, his hand froze. He stared at his unbudging fingers, and the paralysis soaked into his bones, his own body stretched out before him like the map of a foreign land—distant, strange, the legend written in a language he no longer understood.

. . . .

In the dining room, Sherri hustled to keep pace at the bar. Her reprieve had been short-lived, and she was now deluged with orders, requests frequently repeated due to the increasing din. The conjoined Siamese twins requested White Russians, a Sea Breeze for the ballerina. Glass clinked as Sherri pulled out and replaced the bottles, her hand numb from repeated plungings into the cooler's icy water. She lined up four beer bottles and opened them with rapid-fire precision, their caps raining down onto the table. The barrage subsided when the Queen announced that the director of student affairs was about to begin her raw egg juggling routine, and when Sherri looked up from her mixing, she found herself holding a gin and tonic ordered but now forgotten by an udder-dangling cow.

Mesmerizing, the bubbling streams that filtered between the cubes, the clear liquid in a clear cup, her own warped fingers on the other side. In her dark days, she drank to fill the ever-widening spaces that separated her aspirations from her reality. Love, music, faith—they'd all abandoned her. Alcohol alone had been faithful, a devotion as easy as it was insidious. Now, the drink's gin-lime bite swirled into her head, and the raw, aching desire it triggered overloaded her circuits and sent her into a dazed shutdown. The cup's rim expanded, a creeping boundary that slowly absorbed her, and in her thoughts, the party's clamor receded into an indistinct hum, the cacophony of voices and music and laughter replaced by rattling ice and the ungodly loud *pop-pop-pop* of tiny bubbles.

Liquid spilled over her hand as she set down the drink. Her thigh bumped the table's corner, her tip cup overturned on her escape from behind the makeshift bar. "Sherri?" Amy called, but Sherri ignored her and plunged ahead, a reeling, weak-kneed path through the party throng. Shivers rippled across her shoulders and chest, an unconscious blanching brought on by the room's heady, drunken bouquet, the beckoning odors assaulting her with every costumed jostle. She wove her way into the dimly lit hallway.

Before the guests had arrived, she'd been down here to use the bathroom, but now she stopped short and paused outside a door collaged with a child's artwork. She didn't notice the man in the shaggy wig until she'd shut the door behind her. A cheap guitar rested on his lap, and he clenched the fret board with a white-knuckled intensity.

"Oh," she stammered, "I'm sorry."

"You OK?" he asked.

"Fine, fine." She leaned with her back pressed against the door. "Just needed to clear my head." Her legs still trembling, she sat opposite him on a small, red chair. "Thought changing scenery to a kid's room might help."

Her sudden appearance had broken the crippling spell, and he strummed the guitar. "I'm supposed to be practicing."

"'Classical Gas,' I heard." Reaching out, she turned one of the pegs. "Try that."

He strummed again. "Thanks." He laughed bitterly. "I can't play it. I mean I could once, but now—"

"They'll be happy with anything you play. Half of them have probably forgotten about you already."

"I guess that's comforting."

"How about loosening up with a song you know first. Something simple."

His fingers trembled as he botched a progression. "I'm coming up blank, I'm afraid."

"How about 'Yesterday?'"

"No."

"'Louie, Louie?'"

He shook his head.

She thought for a moment. "How about 'Amazing Grace?'" She hummed the tranquil opening bars.

The song, one recorded on one of the tapes Dana had made for their drive to Mexico, came to him in a rush. "I could do that."

"Sure you can." She hummed again, and missing notes here and there, he mimicked her lead.

"Can we start again?" he asked.

She sang this time instead of humming, her performance drawn out to encourage his trailing accompaniment. *"Amazing grace, how sweet the sound. . ."* Twice she temporarily abandoned the lyrics to offer perfectly pitched instructions, but by the second verse, Tim's playing was smoother, his fingers reacting to the sounds in his head, each note supported on the tide of Sherri's rich voice. The last notes lingered beneath the room's high ceiling then dissipated like an exhaled breath on an icy night.

Sherri wrapped her arms around her shins and rested her chin atop her knees. "That was nice."

Tim squeezed the pick into his palm. "Don't know if I can go out there."

She studied his ashen face, the pained blue eyes that avoided her gaze. "Come on." She stood and, taking his hand in hers, helped him to his feet. "We'll change the playlist and perform together."

With her in the lead, they exited the room. Slices of party activity played out at the far end of the shadowy hallway. Twice the guitar struck the plaster wall, a pair of hollow twangs they alone heard.

"Ah," Paige exclaimed, "our troubadours have returned."

Dave finished mopping the raw egg goo hatched during the juggling act. "Dylan, Hendrix, and now Tim." He guided Tim to a kitchen chair and patted him squarely on the back. "I'm proud of you, my boy. The kingdom is thirsting for talent beyond the carnival midway."

Tim caught Dana standing at the crowd's edge. Paul whispered in her ear, and Dana, a drink raised to her lips, studied Tim over the rim of her glass.

"We need another chair," Tim said absently.

"No need." Sherri knelt by his side.

A hush settled over the room. Sherri gave Tim's arm a quick, tender squeeze, drew a deep breath and began to sing. Tim fell in a half-bar behind. Sherri's voice, aching, sweet, and low, filled the room, and spurred by her performance, Tim played better, too.

With a simple act, they'd pushed back the fears and demons that had hounded them into a child's abandoned room. In the second chorus, Tim surprised them both when he joined her, and by the third, everyone was singing, an untuneful, happy stew of drunken voices.

"More! More!" Dave and the others cheered when the song ended. The lit matches and lighters they raised shed a starshine glow. Tim glanced up but was unable to see Dana.

Sherri leaned toward Tim, her lips brushing his ear. "How's that for a moment of departure?"

Caravan

A ngela sat in the backseat of her parents' packed-to-bursting van. Stacked boxes of dried fruits and shotgun shells cut her little brother from view. He was probably sleeping, which was fine with Angela, the tears he'd been blubbering all morning finally silenced. "Sparky?" Angela whispered, not wanting to wake her brother. Sparky, the family's excitable terrier, scrambled his way from the abandoned passenger seat and clambered onto Angela's lap.

"Good boy," she whispered, stroking the locks framing the dog's dewy, black eyes. She reached into her windbreaker pocket, retrieved a stick of her father's venison jerky and snapped off a brittle chunk. "Sit," she said. Her treat-holding hand rose, a coaxing which lured the dog's front paws from her lap, a trembling, begging pose he held until his jaws snapped the jerky from her fingers. They repeated the ritual a half dozen times until the stick was gone. Satisfied, Sparky hopped over a water purifier and a collection of various-sized rubber boots before settling back into the passenger seat.

Fog pressed in upon the vans and pickups collected in the community center's lot. Like most of the other vehicles, a hitched trailed weighed down their van's rear. Angela's parents and the other adults, their forms whittled to indistinct shadows, stood on the dewy baseball field beside the lot, their heads lowered, their hands linked in prayer. In the circle's center, the prophet raised his arms, and the sleeves of his robe hung like the wings of a bird yearning to take flight. The circle broke, and the adults moved in an uncalled square dance, a reeling from couple to couple, exchanges of hugs and handshakes and kisses. Angela cracked her window and listened to the sounds of their laughter, the women's impromptu singing of "Swing Low, Sweet Chariot" as they emerged from the fog. Strange, Angela thought, rolling up her window, the morning's mood, a twisted Christmas, the adults giddy and euphoric, the children shrinking into the background, quiet observers who understood this was not their day.

Back in the car, her father started the engine, her mother still humming as Sparky curled onto her lap. With a strained groan, the car crept forward. The piled-high provision beside Angela shifted. She braced the seat's cardboard divide, not wanting the boxes to topple onto her brother. Her father took his place in the procession of taillight-flashing vehicles, a caravan of believers. Like the others ahead of them, they paused at the lot's exit.

Angela's father rolled down his window. The morning's chill reached into the car. Goosebumps rose on the bare skin of Angela's arms. From her perspective in the seat directly behind her father, all she could see was the prophet's torso. She studied the faded stain on the robe's front—ketchup, gravy perhaps—and when he laid his hands on the roof to bless the car and their journey, his billowing sleeve exposed the checkered flannel shirt he often wore to their youth group meetings. As her father put the car in gear, the prophet rested his palm against Angela's window. The meat of his hand turned white, and the ghostly impression of lines and calluses lingered on the glass after he'd pulled away. Angela studied him through the smudged impression. She recalled the weight of that hand, its gentle yet insistent pressure as it pried apart her knees the night her parents were late picking her up from Bible study. "My beautiful, obedient lamb," he whispered, his stubbly cheek burning against hers.

Eight weeks ago, on a sticky-warm Sunday of early September, the prophet had declared the time had come. Halleluiah! Angela's focus had not been on the prophet's sermon but on the bright sunshine outside the windows, a white butterfly flitting between the last daylily blooms, her reverie shattered by the adults leaping to their feet, the community center's folding chairs clattering to the floor, the room blossoming with tearful exaltations of joy. Halleluiah, brothers and sisters! The next day, the buying and selling frenzy began. FOR SALE signs sprouted on the congregation's lawns. Angela's family made nightly trips to The Home Depot, and when they stumbled upon other believers in the cavernous aisles, the adults broke into public scenes of barely contained ecstasy, their heaven-praising hands raised to the store's girdered ceiling. The cashiers joked with them at first, but as the weeks passed, they simply eyed them with increasing suspicion as their checkout scanners chirped. The believers sold their houses, a glut on the market in which few received their asking price, but none of them bothered to haggle, the buyers' initial offers pounced upon for Angela's family and the rest of the flock were headed to a shimmering future where faith would be the only currency that mattered.

On the main road, their trailer rattled behind them. An overblown breadbox balanced on two wheels, the trailer was packed tight with axes and shovels, firearms and ammunition, ropes, a pair of machetes, lanterns, a generator, casting nets, rice and flour in twenty-pound sacks, waterproof matches, clothes that would see Angela and her brother through puberty, enough vegetable seeds to sustain a murder of crows. Angela had helped her father pack the trailer, a chore that seemed haphazard at first but soon transformed into an intricate puzzle, Angela perched atop her father's shoulders, the final box of canned pears wedged into a ceiling-scraping nook. When they bolted the trailer door, Angela thought it was all more than necessary, her father's typical overkill. Now, as they passed through the sluggish hush of town, their only company the pre-breakfast dog walkers and huffing joggers, she felt horribly unprepared, naked in a way that had nothing to do with clothes.

How would the end come? The Lord had given the prophet

the gift of the hour but had withheld His means. The elders debated whether the wicked would perish in fire or ice, nuclear war or plague or drought. These conversations struck Angela as both morbid and peculiar, the adults willingly divorcing themselves from the only reality they'd ever known, the actuality of flesh just a footnote to the rapture that awaited their saved souls. The prophet's last few sermons had hedged from such images of annihilation, hinting that what awaited the outside world may be a fate which kept bodies and cities intact but which would drown the disbelievers in a flood of pornography and greed and Godless humanism. One way or another, the prophet claimed his flock would be spared, be it in the next world of God's kingdom or in this one, all of them safe in their fortified compound high in the hills.

Angela rested her hand against the window. The fading imprint the prophet had left dwarfed her outstretched fingers. They passed her school, the library. The football stadium and the playground and the movie theater. They'd never return—this was the only solid truth Angela could cling to, and she focused on this lone, immutable nugget until it hardened in the pit of her belly. With this knowledge, everything outside her window faded to dust, vaporized, consumed not only by the fog but also by a world-leveling magic worthy of the Old Testament and the promises of Revelations. Halleluiah.

"Silence is golden, my lamb," the prophet had whispered, his breath smelling of half-chewed meat and damp forests. In the front seat, her mother hummed the opening notes of "I Shall Be Released." Her father joined in on the second verse, and Sparky yowled a piercing, tail-wagging accompaniment. They passed Angela's best friend's house, the one with the creaking porch swing Angela loved, a laundry chute which rose like a hollow tree through the house's innards. Angela turned, watching the house fade into the mist, and she wondered how long her friend and all the others in town would remember them. When would their flock be swallowed by the drudgery of uncounted days, by the milestones of birthdays and funerals, weddings and graduations? Perhaps only then would Angela and the others in their caravan become what the prophet had promised they'd soon all be, spirits released from this world.

Marik, the Rapist

Marik Boyko was raised on a pig farm outside the village of Lvivska, a crossroads dot on the Ukrainian steppe. Wheat fields engulfed Lvivska, tan oceans alive with wind-rippled waves. What little notoriety the village enjoyed came from its proximity to the Great Peoples' Dam on the Desna River. Marik's mother died giving birth to her first child, a tragedy for which his father never forgave him. The boy grew up familiar with the snap of his father's belt, his backside crisscrossed with welts, his nights often spent in the barn loft where the grunts of huddled pigs took the place of bedtime stories and lullabies.

Marik and his father survived the purges and reforms and famines of the '30's. Marik attended the village school until the age of twelve. His teachers judged him a lazy and hopelessly dull child, his father's beatings often echoed by his masters' ear pullings and paddlings, punishments which, after the pitiless bruisings inflicted by his father, barely fazed Marik. One of the older girls took pity on the boy with the pig shit-stinking boots and the narrow eyes that never cried, and at recess, she'd sit with him, using sticks to draw numbers and letters in the schoolyard dirt, but the boy showed neither the aptitude nor the desire to learn.

After he left school, his classmates would see him in town from time to time. He grew, his pants no longer reaching his ankles, his coat so tight it pinched his broadening shoulders. While his father bartered with the local merchants, Marik herded his pigs with stinging lashes of his whip or loaded a cart pulled by their team of sickly oxen. Sometimes his old mates or the girl who had tutored him at recess would say hello, but Marik barely nodded in reply before returning to his cart or pigs.

In the summer of '41, the war came. The newspaper accounts of heroic defenses were undercut by the retreating armies that rolled through town, the tanks and trucks, mechanized monsters that spat oily clouds and rattled pictures from the walls. In their wake came the men on foot, ragtag and somber legions, their march often halted at the village square's stone fountain. Here, the soldiers quenched their thirst and rubbed handfuls of water over their dirt-streaked faces. The townspeople studied these men, taking currency in the silent shock of their eyes, and soon after the soldiers had marched off, the people of Lvivska began to imitate the soldiers' westward gaze, their eyes fixed on a vast horizon now spotted by tendrils of rising black smoke.

On the day news of Kiev's fall reached town, a trio of trucks rolled into the square. Army officers armed with megaphones and pistols patrolled the streets, shouting orders for all men to gather by the fountain, the reluctant ones hurried along with gunshots fired into the air. The shops emptied, the granary's flour-coated workers marched out, their eyes blinking in the midday sun. The women watched from a distance, fearful, many sobbing. The officers marched up and down the line, the men asked what they did for a living then judged the way a farmer judges his livestock, those too infirm or young pushed roughly aside, the vast majority herded into the trucks. Marik, who'd happened to be in town to buy salt and vodka for his father, was whisked away with the others.

Later that night, the village's party officials and police force made their own exodus, and in their absence, a queer hush settled over town, a sense of stalled time and uncertain fates. White sheets billowed from the churches' steeples and from the electric lines linking town to the dam. The granary's doors swung open, an unwritten invitation that had all of Lvivska hauling flour home in buckets and pots, and the sweet aroma of baking bread flavored the warm evenings. In the streets, children played soccer with the balls of bundled rag strips stitched together by Vanya the tailor. For three days, the people of Lvivska lived like this, ghosts unclaimed by any nation, until the afternoon the Germans rolled into town.

No shots were fired, an initial gesture which bolstered the belief of some that the Germans would liberate them from the hated Russians, a notion swiftly dispensed after Sasha the banker was shot dead as he approached the invaders with gifts of flowers and wine. From sunrise to sundown the columns thundered past, majestic Panzers and platoons in trucks and rattling artillery pieces, the enemy glimpsed from behind drawn curtains as they paused to drink at the fountain. Another week of limbo passed before the occupiers settled in, a brand of soldier the residents of Lvivska found less impressive than the initial wave, some little more than frightened adolescents, others fat and lazy, still others already marred by eye patches and limps and a host of other wounds suffered in distant lands.

The Germans stayed for over two years. In the square, they constructed a gallows and hanged partisans and black marketeers and the schoolhouse teachers. Marik's father and a half dozen others were gunned down in retaliation for a stolen shipment of cognac, a Christmas present intended for the garrison's commander. Old women shivering in line to receive their ration of sawdusty bread soon gave little notice to the blue-faced victims twisting at the ropes' ends. Yet despite the ever-present threat of brutality, a workaday rhythm soon claimed them. Crops were harvested, pigs slaughtered, babies conceived and born. The townspeople grew so accustomed to their occupiers that they picked up on their nervous, eastward glances that came that second German spring, a silent gesture that confirmed the rumors that the war's tide had turned. Soon the fires sprouted in the distance, and then the fighting, the Germans less willing to budge than the Russians. Gosha the barber cheered the first incoming rounds of

Katyusha rockets, but he and the rest soon understood shrapnel didn't discriminate between German flesh and Ukrainian. The sea of fractured stones only strengthened the German defenses, the village relinquished one bloody street at a time, the granary transformed into a fortress which the rearguard held to its last man. In retreat, the Germans set fires and booby traps, herded civilians toward the Russian lines, many cut down by their own countrymen as they waved makeshift flags of surrender.

For three days, the battle raged, and when the shooting finally stopped, the survivors of Lvivska climbed from their hiding places. Bodies littered the streets, corpses rigid and burnt, a feast for the crows. Gone was the church that had stood since the days of Peter, its mosaics and icons and golden dome—all of it reduced to ashes. Gone were the newspaper office and bicycle shop and the central market, and the places fortunate enough to remain bore scars ranging from broken windows to missing roofs. A crowd gathered around the fountain, its waters now sullied by dust and stones. Fydor the butcher broke out the bottle of vodka he'd been saving for this day, but before he could crack the seal, they were distracted by a distant yet weighty explosion, one that shook their bones and rippled the earth beneath their feet.

The Germans had demolished The Great Peoples' Dam.

Another year passed before the war ended. Most of the men rounded up before the Germans arrived never came home. Women mourned the news of husbands and sons fallen in a hundred towns between Moscow and Berlin. Other men returned with crutches or empty, pinned-back sleeves or head wounds that left them as simple as children. Squatters claimed the Boykos' farm, assuming that Marik, like so many others, had perished in the maelstrom.

On a cool winter-hinting day in the autumn of '45, a pack of children sprinted into the square. "A jeep's coming!" they yelled. Their skinny arms pointed up the road. Fydor the butcher, Gosha the barber and his lather-cheeked customer, and all the others who'd reclaimed their shops and repaired them as best they could stepped outside in time to witness an army jeep bucking to a halt alongside the fountain. His drab olive chest festooned with glimmering medals, Marik Boyko, now with a chin of rough stubble and the build of a bear, stepped onto the cobblestone street in the same spot from which he'd been swept into the war's tide over four years before. Before speeding away, the captain who'd accompanied him climbed onto the jeep's hood and addressed the crowd: "People of Lvivska, I bring home your son, the war hero Marik. He has been appointed by the party to be your new police chief."

Marik, with his wide, flat face, his jutting brow that cast shadows over his eyes, surveyed his surroundings. In one hand, he carried a suitcase, and tucked protectively under his other arm, a wooden box whose front was adorned with dials and knobs, a burden he shielded from the approaching crowd with twists of his bulky torso and grunted threats. In Lev's bar, the village men bought him rounds of vodka and all the dumplings he could eat, and in return, Marik, in a graveled voice that reminded the older men of his father, told of battles and blood, of being among the first shock troops to storm the Reichstag.

With him, Marik had brought home a noticeable limp, a medal pinned on by Stalin himself, a radio he'd purchased at a party store in Moscow, and unbeknownst to all, an appetite for rape.

The gravel and packed-dirt road that led from Lvivska was the only overland route to the eastern shore of The Great Peoples' Dam. As a child, Marik often woke in the barn loft to the distant thunder of dynamite or the stampede of truck caravans, the turning wheels which kicked up a fine, gritty haze that dulled the morning sun. Crews erected poles and linked them with lines, the wires radiating out, a spider's web over the flatlands.

The people of Lvivska huddled in the November cold to witness the first streetlamp's lighting. "What an age we live in," Vanya said to Fydor as they lingered in the lamp's glow. In time, more lines were hung, a charged splintering of swaying wires. Fydor installed a freezer, and the lamps in the ten-bed hospital burned through the long winter nights. Despite the threat of public floggings, men tapped into the lines without the proper permits, the potential punishment overshadowed by the thrill of having a bulb illuminate a closet large enough to hold a chair or a room where blankets sealed off the windows.

That spring it became popular to take a Sunday and travel the four kilometers to picnic along the newly formed shores of The Peoples' Lake. The men fished while the women tended fires, and after their meals, the families would often hike to the dam itself, awed by the curving grace of the gray concrete monolith, by the precipitous drop to the swirling waters below.

During the occupation, the power lines became a point of contention between the Germans and the partisans. The partisans would hack down a pole, the electricity in town lost for a day or two before the Germans performed their repairs. In the interim, suspected sympathizers were rounded up, beaten and interrogated, sometimes hung. When the Germans left, they took foodstuffs and livestock, their files emptied and burned in the courtyard behind their headquarters. They also ripped out every bit of wiring and dynamited scores of poles between the village and the dam. The Russians reclaimed a city in ruins, the collaborators summarily shot, the boys who'd come of age during the occupation given guns and issued uniforms often marred by bullet holes and blood stains.

In the months to follow, the wheat was sown and harvested and sown again. Children played games with the shell casings they collected, and three farmers were killed in separate incidents when their plows struck unexploded mines. On the day the news came of Berlin's fall, a band played in the square, women danced and the men drank until they stumbled home. The church bell, salvaged from the rubble of its centuries-old home and then hidden by the priest who'd feared the Russians would melt it for bullets, rang for the first time in years. The summer passed, a cautious euphoria, and fall saw the return of Marik, the hero and Lvivska's new police chief.

. . . .

That winter, a state-sponsored band of traveling entertainers trundled into Lvivska. They set up in the workers' hall, the structure which had been the town's synagogue at the turn of the century. The building's roof was new, but the windows had yet to arrive. Wind hissed between the wooden shutters nailed over the openings, and in a room that still smelled of fresh plaster, the waiting crowd shivered in their hats and coats, their stamping feet staving off the chill. Hoots rose from the audience, calls for the show to start, the collected steam of their breath misting in the gas lamps' yellow glow, but when the lights dimmed and the generator kicked on, all fell silent. On stage, two members of the troupe held a bed sheet, and on its rippling surface, black and white images played, newsreels of the Red Army marching amid the rubble of Berlin. In the front row, Marik sat forward, entranced.

Other shorts followed—Stalin and his ever-changing henchmen overlooking a Red Square procession, ice skaters performing twists and leaps, a circus parade, the national wrestling competitions. After the last tail of film sputtered through the projector and the lights were turned up, the actors—four young men and one woman in a severe haircut—took the stage. The actors juggled and tumbled and rode unicycles, routines of daring slapstick before they settled into a series of morality skits, each with its own message—the evils of hoarding and profiteering, the inherent rewards of comradeship and hard labor. After the actors took their bows, the party official who'd accompanied them stepped onto the wooden rise that was once the synagogue's bimah. In a rumbling, theatric baritone, he delivered an impassioned speech extolling the Soviet people's glorious victory over fascism. Tears streaked his cheeks as he detailed the sacrifices of Leningrad, his voice rising to a bone-quivering thunder as he recounted the triumph of Kursk.

"And in ending tonight, good people of Lvivska, I bring you a promise from our great leader himself." He paused, a smile lifting the corner of his mouth and his eyes taking in the room. "He personally asked me to tell the good citizens of Lvivska that come spring we will rebuild The Great People's Dam!"

He nodded and the lanterns were dimmed. From outside came the fitful lurch of the troupe's generator. An electric filament flickered in the bulb the speaker held from a dangling wire. His face basked in harsh illumination, he held the wire high above his head, the bulb waving pendulum-like, his face crossed with shifting shadows. "Long live the People's Socialist Republic!" he bellowed. "Long live our great father, Comrade Stalin!"

In the first row, Marik leapt to his feet. His meaty hands thunder-clapped, and his narrow eyes turned back to the audience as he took inventory of those who didn't display the same level of enthusiasm, a subtle intimidation that ensured the applause went on and on. Backstage, Anya, Dasha and Katenka, the town prostitutes, watched from the wings, their entrance secured with a two-minute favor imparted to the hall's manager. When the meeting let out, the women slipped back into the night, hoping to conduct their business without encountering Marik.

Anya sprinted down the alley behind the central market. Behind her, Marik's gravel-kicking limp, a spasmodic rhythm that fueled Anya's panic. Dogs howled, the alley cats hissed, and the misty parcels of Anya's breath rose into a chilled, star-speckled sky. Anya scrambled over the rubble heap that was once the home of the village blacksmith, toppling trash bins in her wake, hoping to distance herself from Marik. At the edge of the fountain square, she paused and listened for his labored grunts, the telltale thump-scrape of his footfalls. Believing she'd lost him, she set off, but at the next alley crossing, a paw-like hand clamped over her mouth and wrestled her back into the shadows.

Since returning, Marik had limited his rapes to the town's prostitutes. After the second, Kostya the pimp made the miscalculation of approaching Marik, a plea not for money but for a bit of a less heavy-handed treatment of his girls. The beating Marik unleashed left Kostya with two less teeth and no stomach for dealing with Marik again. The girls would have lain with him just to avoid the village jail, but instead Marik chose to brutalize them, the girls returning to Kostya sore and dazed, their eyes blackened and ribs cracked. Staggering from the west end bars, Marik would hunt down Anya or fiery Dasha or simple Katenka. There had been a fourth, Elena the beautiful mute and her bastard German child, but no one had seen them for weeks. Katenka believed Elena and her child had left to start anew in Kharkiv, a contention Dasha openly scoffed, saying Marik no doubt murdered mother and child and fed their bodies to the pigs he now kept in the pen behind his house at the edge of town.

Marik shoved Anya to the dirt of an alley trash stall and fell upon her before she could crawl away. Vodka burned on his breath, his curses rasping and harsh. He yanked out a fistful of her hair by the roots. The scent of pigs clung to his coat. He ripped her underwear, yanked down his pants, and entered her with a painful thrust.

"Marik, don't you remember me—"

"Shut up," he said. His hand closed around her throat, a windpipe squeeze to remind her how delicate a hold she had on life.

The dam reconstruction began in earnest with the spring thaw. A new home was built on the town's east side for the project's engineer, an owl-faced man who kept to his books and papers. Caravans once again rolled through Lvivska, a river of supplies and men, war prisoners mostly, and in town, it became sport to pelt the hated Germans with stones and rotten potatoes, to splash them with urine or pig shit. But by mid-summer, the spectacle only managed to hold the children's attention, the adults' rage tempered by the prisoners' unresponsiveness, by the dull sheen of death in their eyes. What point was there in taunting a ghost?

Once a month, the party members gathered in the workers' hall. The meeting that August was the first for the generator Marik had secured with a bribe to one of the convoy drivers, and the machine's purrs rippled through the night air. Inside, the bulbs' unflinching white lit the recently installed windows, and the shine spilled out, dry puddles on the cobblestones.

Marik, his hesitant boot scraping as he strode down the street's center, neared the hall. Under his arm, he carried his radio, and for the moment, Anya and Dasha and Katenka felt safe, knowing Marik would never put his most precious possession in jeopardy by chasing them down. For the next few hours, the women patrolled the alleys and backstreets, but business was slow with the party members already occupied. After midnight, before the women returned to Kostya to divvy up their earnings, Anya and the others paused beneath the window at the hall's rear. A block of scrap wood propped up the window, the burning tobacco scent drifting out, but a hush had replaced the usual din. Anya stilled her breath and listened, and like a thread in the fabric of the near silence, out came a woman's voice, a sung tale of lost love. Anya had heard Marik boast his radio could pick up the signal from Kiev, even Donetsk if the night was clear.

"Put your hands together, like this," Anya whispered to Dasha and Katenka. They imitated the stirrup she'd created with interlaced fingers and upward-facing palms. Anya placed a shoe in each offered set of hands, and when she nodded, the women slowly lifted her until Anya was able to peek inside.

Bottles littered the long table where the men sat, the picked-to-the-bone remnants of their feast as yet uncleared. Marik hunkered at the near end of the table, his broad back to the window, and just over his shoulder, Anya spied the radio, its dial's halo-shine seeming to cast a spell over the dozen or so men huddled nearby. Anya lingered for a moment, studying Marik's downward gaze, a pose that reminded her of the way he'd sit by her side as she scratched words in the schoolyard dirt.

A leafless willow branch in hand, Marik herded a pig to Fydor's butcher shop. The branch whistled as Marik delivered blows to the pig's hide, the *thwaks* and grunts a counterpoint to rhythmic procession of hooves over the cobblestones. Marik entered the square to find a commotion already in progress. At the far end of the fountain sat a farmer's ox cart. The farmer had climbed from his perch, and at the front, he pulled the team's reigns, yelling and urging, but the oxen refused to budge. Behind the cart, a truck carrying German laborers idled, and the driver leaned from the window, cursing the oxen and the farmer.

Anya and Dasha, each carrying wicker baskets of laundry, entered the square, then pulled back at the sight of Marik, huddling in an alcove's shadows as the scene played out in the square. Others now joined the overwhelmed farmer and the impatient truck driver, Vanya the tailor and Alexi the cobbler, even Petya, the legless veteran who'd rolled his squeaking dolly to the oxen, his muscular arms waving, his callused hands clapping in an attempt to stir the stubborn beasts. Marik stepped forward to investigate, and his hog wandered to the fountain, its snout poking over the edge as it slurped.

"A pig for a fucking pig," Dasha whispered. The two women worked the same trade, but Dasha was born to be a woman of the streets, if not a prostitute then a con artist or a fleece or pickpocket. Anya had been a student in Kiev in the spring of '41. As the Germans neared, she hiked and begged rides on her journey back to Lvivska, but she returned to an empty house. The note left on the kitchen table said her mother had taken her younger sister east, while her father had headed to Kiev to find her. Anya would never see them again, and when the Germans came, they claimed her house for officers' quarters, throwing Anya to the street. Hungry and alone, she soon fell in with Kostya the pimp, her slim waist and green eyes translating into the most primal of currencies.

Behind the truck, a passel of schoolchildren hurled pebbles at the listless Germans. The Germans faced each other on long planks on either side of the truck's bed, and a tall one seated at the truck's rear began to scold the children and shush them away, his hands gesturing for them to move along. He wore round glasses, one lens missing, the other cracked. Perhaps, Anya thought, he'd been a schoolmaster in his old life, one who needed glasses to grade his students' papers, a man who expected better behavior from children.

Marik turned from the melee at the truck's front and strode to the rear. He barked at the children, swatting and kicking the laggards who hadn't heeded his order to step back. He turned to the German and, grabbing a fistful of dirty uniform, pulled him roughly from the truck. The wire rim glasses fell, the remaining lens crunched beneath the German's boot as he staggered forward. With a swift set of motions, Marik unsnapped the clasp on his leather holster, took out his revolver and fired a single round into the man's head.

The German went limp, his bones seeming to melt beneath his skin, and collapsed in a heap. The gunshot echoed. The oxen bayed and stirred, the cart's wheels finally turning, the farmer scampering back onto his perch. Blood ran in zigzagging streams between the cobblestones. Marik's pig sniffed the man's mismatched boots. Flecks of skull and steaming droplets of gray matter fanned out from where the man had stood. Marik pointed the gun toward the Germans and gestured for the closest two to retrieve their comrade. "Schnell, schnell," Marik barked, the barrel pressed into the temple of the trembling man carrying the bloody upper body. The men threw their comrade into the bed then climbed aboard. The truck slipped into gear with a shudder and rolled away. Marik grabbed his willow branch and smacked his pig then, with stick raised, threatened the children until they scattered.

Dasha turned to Anya and hissed, "He should die."

In the kitchen of the house the women shared with Kostya, Anya and Dasha tended to Katenka. A candle burned on the kitchen table, another in the dining room where Kostya sat, his long knife whittling a block of wood. Mud and straw sullied Katenka's long, blond hair. Anya twisted a cloth, a rainy drip into a wash basin, the water tinted pink. In the distance, another dynamite blast from the dam. The candle's flame twitched.

"Funny thing is, the big cut—" Katenka cringed as she attempted to point to the gash on her forehead, "the big cut I didn't get from him. I got it running from him. Fell right on my face."

Dasha stood behind her, a comb in hand as she picked a dirty tuft from Katenka's beautiful mane. "Don't make excuses for the fiend."

Anya wrung out the cloth. "What did he do then?"

Katenka looked perplexed. "He got on top of me."

"Swine," Anya said, and Katenka winced as Anya resumed her dabbing.

Kostya's knife dug into the block of wood. "Any other man and I'd slit his throat."

"But not him, right?" Dasha snapped.

Kostya stood and brushed the curled shavings from his lap. He wiped the knife, the same knife Anya had seen him stick into the eye of the lecherous mutant Dimitri, against the thigh of his pants. "I could never get close enough." He closed the knife, set it on the table, and stared at Anya with an intentness that gave his words the feeling of a close-passing hunk of river ice, their depth and weight hidden far below the surface. "No man could get that close."

The theater troupe returned late that fall. Posters now adorned the hall—slogans extolling the redeeming qualities of labor, images of healthy women and wide-shouldered men, their chins lifted proudly and their eyes set on the distance. The townspeople gathered on the room's long benches, the latecomers forced to stand, Petya and his metal-wheeled dolly up front. The children scampered about until they were corralled by their elders with ear tugs and swatted behinds. Up front, in the spot once the home to the ark and its sash-bound scrolls, hung a giant, lording portrait of Stalin.

Outside, Anya, Dasha and Katenka took turns standing atop the rickety pile of crates they'd erected beneath the back window, their only companions the alley cats and the troupe's driver, a white-haired man who cursed as he struggled with the company's apparently ailing generator. Inside, a juggler kept six eggs in the air without cracking one. The comics and illusionists drew laughter and gasps. Between skits, the entertainers led rounds of patriotic songs, the party members' voices rising above the rest, a crowing competition in the barnyard of Soviet loyalty.

The troupe's leader took the stage. For a long moment, he said nothing, only surveyed the crowd with a smile on his face. "Comrades," he said finally, his voice carrying, "I stand before you this evening with glorious news. The reconstruction of The Great People's Dam has been completed!" His applause was echoed by those in the room, an ovation accompanied by stomping feet, shrill whistles. Up front, Marik stood, his waving arms urging the others to follow his lead. "All hail our great leader, Comrade Stalin! All hail the Soviet People's Republic!"

The lights dimmed, and the troupe leader's voice reached out of the darkness. "Soon the town of Lvivska will be awash in light!"

Outside, the juggler had joined the driver in his struggles with the generator, but their cord pulls yielded only sputtering failure.

The leader's voice came again, louder this time, agitated. "Soon the town of Lvivska will be awash in light!"

Another cord pull, the juggler now fiddling with a screwdriver. The generator's coughing attempts gelled into a hoarse growl. Inside, the string of hung electric lights flashed then settled into a steady glow. Anya studied Marik, his broad face turned to the ceiling lights, his usual scowl softened to the pleased expression of a child holding a new toy.

In the early hours of a Sunday morning, Anya and Katenka sat at the kitchen table as they divided the evening's take with Kostya. A candle shed a waxy glow just bright enough for Anya to shave the mold from the block of cheese they shared. True, the dam had been completed, but the promise of electricity had been delayed, the town's infrastructure still in disrepair. Once a week, a delivery truck arrived from Kiev, a trickle of wiring and connectors and switches that ensured electricity would only arrive a house or two at a time. Kostya poured them each a sliver of vodka, then retreated to his bed in an adjoining room.

Dasha entered not long after Kostya began snoring. She sat tenderly, sniffing back tears. When she emptied her purse's coins onto the table, the others saw the scratches on her hands. Anya cut her a slice of cheese and Katenka tore a hunk of bread. Dasha ate with wincing care, the balled portion of her half-chewed food shifted to the side opposite her swollen cheek.

"Are you OK?" Katenka asked finally.

Dasha slammed her fist against the table. The coins jumped. She wiped the tear running down her cheek, a glistening swatch over her discolored skin. She reached down and pulled a long knife from her boot and laid it on the table. Candlelight glimmered along the blade. "I couldn't do it." She sniffed back her tears. "I thought I could, but when my chance came, I froze, too scared to do anything but lay there." She poured a glass of vodka and downed it with a shudder.

They sat in silence until Katenka said: "I saw Anton's house has electricity now."

"Anton," Dasha huffed. "Anton and Marik and all the other party scum. Of course they come first. They should die. All of them should die, all the way up to Stalin, the king of the pigs."

Katenka held a finger to her lips. "Don't say such things, Dasha.

It's good you didn't stab him," Anya said. "You'd hang if you were lucky enough to kill him."

Katenka perked up. "We could poison him."

"Yes," Dasha scoffed, "do that the next time you're cooking for him."

"I don't want to hang." Katenka rubbed her neck. "I saw a man hang once and his head popped off, just like a doll's head."

Anya rubbed Katenka's shoulder. "Don't worry. We wouldn't let that happen to you."

Marik threw Anya to the cold dirt of the priest's rectory garden. Brittle corn stalks lay bent and snapped around her. The priest's cat watched from atop the garden fence, his eyes impassive, his tail faintly twitching. Anya twisted, hurled dirt in Marik's face, attempted to thrust her knee into his groin, but her will to fight withered with each endured slap, her thoughts dimming as Marik squeezed her throat. He pried her legs apart, and as he wriggled fitfully out of his pants, she surrendered to the brutish weight brought down upon her.

"Bitch," he grunted. Spit flew from his lips. "Fucking bitch, fucking bitch."

She turned to him, his wide, ugly face blotting out the sky, a threatening moon glaring down on her and those she loved. She sucked a deep breath and tried to ease her clenched muscles, accepting again his humiliation, his heartless rage. The image of him as a child rose into her thoughts. She'd taken pity on him because he'd wear the same gray shirt for days on end, because on the rare occasions he spoke, he refused to lift his eyes from his scraped shoes. One day in the schoolyard, after another paddling from his teacher, he laid his head on her lap, and in a faint, sobbing whisper, he called her "Mother." She stroked his greasy hair as his breathing settled, the word *mother* repeated in bird-like coos until the headmaster rang his bell. The war had changed them all, but perhaps, Anya thought, none more than Marik. Without the war, she doubted he'd have discovered his talent for murder and savagery. He would have remained a simple pig farmer. Nothing more, nothing less.

He slapped her so hard her teeth clamped together, her tongue bitten. "Bitch. Fucking bitch," he huffed. His cap tumbled onto her face, a momentary blindness. The metallic flavor of blood trickled down her throat.

With the next slap, Anya fell away from the moment, a retreat from the pain of the flesh, her notion of self sinking far beneath her skin. Marik's motions reminded Anya of the way her mother had churned butter, and in her gut, another type of hardening, the realization of what she must do, a realization which grew more certain with each bruising thrust. Marik's labors ascended into a disgusting frenzy. Anya latched onto his shoulders and hooked her feet around his legs, a tentacle-wrapping embrace that gave a brief pause to his attack. Anya opened her mouth and let the air escape her lungs in an imitation of a moan, a liar's charade sung into his ear as he heaved one last time and collapsed on her chest.

He rolled off her, and together, they sat on the chilled earth and arranged their clothes. Clouds of their calming breath plumed above their heads. Before Marik could stand, Anya spoke: "Do you think I could hear your radio?"

He snorted. "You come to my house?"

"Just a few minutes. It's late. No one will see me."

He stood, the wide bulk of him blocking the sky as he finished securing his buckles and buttons. "Follow if you want."

They walked back into the night, Anya observing a twenty-meter buffer, her stride over recently poured concrete and centuries-old cobblestones slowed to mimic his foot-dragging limp. A deep, accepting peace found her for she understood that, for one of them, this was their last walk. Marik entered his house at the edge of town and turned on the light. Anya circled around back, her shoes clacking over the porch's warped boards. A mouse darted behind the firewood stack. In the adjoining yard, Marik's huddled pigs dozed.

He opened the door and she slipped inside. The greasy scent of cooked bacon hung in the air. A single light burned above the kitchen table, the bulb sheathed in a metal collar. Anya stepped into the cone of white, cowering slightly as if the shine cast an invisible weight upon her shoulders. Marik brushed the caked dirt from his elbow and knees, and when he was done, he opened the stove's grill, stirred the orange-red embers, and tossed in a log. A meat cleaver hung beside the stovepipe. Between the stove and the table sat a metal bathing tub, and on the table rested Marik's prized radio.

Anya pulled a chair to the table. The light's power line had been split, and stretching onto his tiptoes, Marik uncoiled the black cord that hung in loops from a rafter nail. A cumbersome outlet marked the cord's tail. Marik snagged the outlet and plugged in the radio. The dial glowed, a face of concentric, number-bearing circles which radiated out from the center like a series of still-water ripples.

"Move," Marik said.

She rose and he took her seat. The dial's reflection shimmered in the cleaver's wide blade. Marik leaned close and fiddled the tuner through a static sea until he dredged faint nuggets of sound, morsels which he rolled over again and again until he teased out the strain of a violin, then a man's voice reading the news—a mine collapse in Belarus, a record sturgeon caught in the Black Sea. Speakers flanked the dial, and how delicate, the manner in which his meaty fingers picked lint from the speakers' cloth faces, a veneer of gentleness broken when he kicked her foot and warned her to keep her distance.

She sat while he added another log to the fire. What a perplexing place this world could be, its wonders of electricity and its beauties of music counterbalanced by its twisted monsters like Marik. The looping cord lay behind the radio, a length Anya figured was long enough to reach the corners of the room. Marik put a kettle on the stove then took off his jacket. He lifted an arm, smelled his pit, and frowned.

"A bath perhaps?" Anya said, the words leaving her throat before she could consider them. He locked her in a harsh stare, and she swiftly added: "And maybe I could use the water after if it's still warm. I'll prepare it if you'd like."

Marik jammed another log into the stove. The radio's newscast gave way to a symphony. Anya carried a pair of buckets outside, and beneath the frozen starlight, worked the wheezing pump handle. Water spurted from the rusted nozzle, a splashing into the buckets. The pigs stirred, considered her impassively, and returned to their slumber. Smoke rose from the roof's slender chimney, gray flecks of ash that fluttered off like summer moths.

In the tub, she mixed water heated and not, testing it with a swirl of her hand, a blanket draped over the top to seal in the warmth. A drop of scalding water splashed her hand, a heartbeat of pain. The stove's fire crackled.

She poured in another pot. "It's ready."

The radio symphony eased through a lulling adagio. Anya glanced away as Marik unbuttoned his shirt, but she turned back as he stepped out of his pants and stood before her. She hadn't seen him naked before, the marked meat of him, the unaligned kneecap, the white, snaking scars around his torso. As he stepped into the tub, she cupped his elbow, a crutch as his weight shifted to his bad leg. He eased himself down. The water covered his legs and reached up to his waist. He pulled back his feet as she poured a last pot of boiling water into the tub. Steam curled beneath the light's cone.

"There's a cloth by the stove," he said, his thumb gesturing over his shoulder.

The music grew louder, an itching, restless momentum. She picked up the cloth, and with a held breath meant to steady her hand, she slid the cleaver from its hook. She approached the thick shoulders that rose above the tub's rim. She braced herself for the sickening vibration of severed meat and bone which would ride into her, braced herself for the gush of blood and the animal howls Marik would unleash. And she braced herself at an even deeper level, one beyond the moment's initial shock, for she knew the job would require more blows than one.

She stood behind him, and reaching over his shoulder, dropped the cloth into the water. The symphony surged toward its crescendo. Cymbals clashed. Kettle drums rumbled, and the furious tempo swirled in Anya's brain. She stepped back when his hand rose from the tub, his water-dripping fingers unable to reach the radio's dials.

"Turn this up." He pointed to the radio on the table. "That knob."

Anya had always been a good student, attentive and questioning, and she recalled a lesson her teacher had given after the first lights had been installed in town about the dangers of electricity and water. With a lurching sweep of her arm, she pushed the radio off the table and into the tub.

The initial splash was followed by a prolonged fizzle. The light above flickered, a spasmodic pulse, and rising from the water, a thicker, more acrid brand of steam. The cleaver grasped in both hands and held defensively before her, Anya circled to the tub's front. Marik sat at a rigid attention undercut by a network of faintly twitching muscles. Half submerged, the radio rested in his lap, its dial's shine throbbing in time with the light over his head, the water illuminated in dulled flashes. The sound of bees filled the room, a buzz that continued for over a minute until the light died with a shudder. Marik slumped down, sinking a centimeter at a time until his face disappeared beneath the water's surface.

The cleaver slipped from Anya's hands, and its tip bit into the wooden floor. Anya stumbled out the back door and lurched down the porch steps. The chill cut into her. The pigs gathered themselves, and the lot of them moved with a single yet sluggish state of mind, a forward parade fueled by increasingly agitated grunts. The mud sucked at their hooves, and their wet, twitching snouts poked between the pen's fence rails as Anya staggered past.

Running would draw attention, so she pulled her shawl over her head and walked with her eyes fixed on the ground, the dirt and rubble and gravel, the cobblestones as she approached the square. Dogs barked. Cats slinked into shadows and nooks. Her shoes clicked over the stones. In the week to come, she would attend to her business, and once Marik's body was in the ground, she would leave. She would return to Kiev, get a job in a factory or store or office, reenroll at the university if she could, and when she left, she would ask Dasha and Katenka to join her, and if Kostya dared give her trouble, she would suffer his beating then kill him in his sleep, his own knife thrust deep into his heart. Murder, she reasoned, would come easier to a soul already damned.

A transport truck idled alongside the square's fountain. One of the truck's drivers passed through the headlight shine, and he climbed onto the bumper, the hood raised as he poured water into the radiator. Anya walked on the fountain's opposite side, keeping her distance yet close enough to spy into the truck. Beneath the bed's flimsy canvas shelter, a group of laborers shivered. The truck's other driver stood guard, rifle in hand. Inside the truck, only the first few faces were visible, and the nearest, gaunt and blond, a human skeleton she'd assumed was asleep, lifted his chin and stared at her.

In his eyes, Anya sensed the worlds they shared, a wordless communication like two wild animals stumbling upon each other along a quiet stream. They were alike, yes, creatures born into the relentless cycles of hunger and death and brutality. Yet there was a difference between them as vast as the horizon-melting wheat fields that surrounded this town, for while he was doomed, she still had hope, that most precious of all human gifts. Buoyed, she turned and walked a bit faster to the flat she shared with the others. When she arrived, she would tell Dasha and Katenka about Marik, a secret they would promise to take to their graves. She would tell them about the semester she studied in Kiev before the war, the streetcars and cinemas and the ballet, the musicians who played every Friday night along the river. Not even the war could make Dasha and Katenka leave Lvivska, but Anya would try. She would talk until dawn if that's what it took to soften Dasha's distrustful soul, to budge Katenka's stubborn innocence. She would fall asleep in their arms, offering them nothing but all the hope in her heart.

Fever

The whispering drizzle froze the moment it touched the earth. The glaze thickened on the pickup, its metal and chrome mummified beneath a slick, dimpled skin. Marge sat by an opened window in her son's bedroom. Her breath clouded the moment it plumed through the screen. Mesmerizing, the night's queer colors, the darkness given depth by the earth's crystalline sheen, by a sky choked with a million fleeting prisms. In the woods surrounding the house another branch snapped, a gunshot-loud crack. The echo lingered, captured by the ice above and below.

Marge closed the window and settled into the chair beside her son's bed. The lights had been out since sundown, and in the garage, the generator purred, the house whittled back to its simplest heartbeat of furnace and freezer. A candle burned in a glass jar atop the dresser, a shimmering display on the ceiling that reminded Marge of sunlight on a shallow, rocky creek, an image of the world turned upside down. She brushed a single finger through the flyaway strands atop her son's head, a touch so light it barely registered. How easy it was to forget the angel inside him. How easy to forget the delicate details of the face and hands so often blurred by the whirlwind bustle of a four-year-old's days. She dipped a washcloth into a mixing bowl and twisted out a rainstorm of cool drops. The water's surface rippled, a network of overlapping circles. She folded the cloth and tenderly laid it across her son's forehead.

Her boy cried out, a protesting, incoherent syllable, his shoulders and torso writhing. He rolled onto his side, exposing a patch of wrinkled, moist sheets. Fever. As an emergency room nurse, Marge has witnessed scores of fevers, and she sympathized with the chaos no doubt playing in her son's head, his flitting between pained consciousness and warped visions, the internal heat that unhinged the glue of comprehension. Ten miles of twisting, dark roads separated her from the hospital, and Marge knew a night like this would bring a ghastly parade through the ER's doors, bloody gashes and splintered bones, lives forever changed. If his fever reached 104, she'd call the ambulance. Until then, she'd sit tight and see what broke first, the ice storm or the fever.

Outside, another branch fell, this one close enough to rattle the windows. Marge thought of her husband, how he'd left on a night sticky-hot and thick with cricket calls, crushed by his discovery of her affair with an intern as shallow as he was handsome. *Stupid, foolish,* she scolded herself, her heart's delirious yearnings as much a mystery as when she was a teenager . . . a child. She stroked her boy's flushed cheek, tasted the salty residue on her fingertips, and wondered how many nights he would spend trapped in a fever of one sort or another, his bearings undone by a fire within, a flame he could no more explain than he could resist.

She pulled back his T-shirt sleeve and placed a thermometer in his armpit's sweaty nook. The thermometer chirped . . . 101.5 . . . 102.2 . . . 103.1. . . . Outside, the storm continued. The trees, dreaming of summer, groaned beneath the thickening ice.

Without Words

Ambrose frames his mother's carnation-red teapot and snaps another picture. His camera electronically emits a shutter's exaggerated click. Ambrose considers the click, a sound hollow and meaningless and utterly divorced from the camera's functioning. Yet despite its insincerity, the click holds an odd comfort for a man who grew up in a time when cameras really did make such noises.

Ambrose wanders through the rooms that are the settings of his earliest memories. The house is a split-level, a zigzag nesting of floors connected by short stairwells. After his divorce last year, Ambrose and his teenage son Robert moved in with Ambrose's mother, a temporary yet open-ended solution to the problem of keeping Robert in the same school district while also allowing Ambrose to care for his mother after her stroke. A moody adolescent and a mute mother—Ambrose sometimes feels as if he's been cast into a world of familiar strangers.

The sweat Ambrose worked up cutting his mother's lawn cools on his neck. He pauses by the upstairs hallway's family photos: images framed and fading, uncles and aunts and grandparents—his father, dead these past ten years—each a stolen moment of health and youth. Ambrose continues through the house, pausing here, stooping there, struggling to view these deeply etched surroundings as a stranger might. He snaps pictures of the dining room table, the sofa, the television, Clementine, his mother's temperamental tabby. *Click. Click. Click.*

When he's done, Ambrose heads down the hallway past the laundry room. The whirring din from the garage swells in the narrow space. Ambrose opens the door, and the grinder's cry blossoms. Robert's booted feet protrude from beneath what was once Ambrose's mother's Sunday-driving K-car, a boxy relic years older than Robert. Stripped of its plastic and glass, the car rests in a hunched pose, its back wheels perched atop knee-high metal ramps. Orange sparks spit from beneath the car. A gritty metallic haze accents the garage's ancient flavors of oil and gas. The garage's opened door marks the boundary between the dim interior and afternoon's brilliant sunshine.

For the past four months, Robert has been prepping the car for the county fair's demolition derby. The backseat has been unbolted, its padding added inside the driver's-side door. The dash and mirrors have been removed, the carpet and chrome ripped out, the wires for the radio and speakers cut, the battery rewired and secured to the bare, passenger-side floor. The car, denied all adornment, has acquired a Spartan quality, its suburban blandness replaced by an apocalyptic and oddly utilitarian vision. Although he understands little about automobiles, Ambrose has been part of the project since its inception. He's taken pictures, signed the required log sheets, kept track of receipts—all part of the documentation process required by the graduation committee of Robert's new, alternative school. The garage's bone-rattling din sometimes irks Ambrose, yet he is thankful for the absorption and dedication the task has brought out in Robert since his expulsion from his regular high school after the principal discovered a knife in his locker.

Ambrose calls his son's name, but his only answer comes from the grinder's skittery drone. Ambrose flips the light switch. Robert turns off the grinder and slides out upon his dolly. Grime covers his cheeks, and reverse racoonish markings surround his eyes when he removes his safety goggles. He wears baggy jeans and one of a whole drawer full of black T-shirts. The uneven layers of the mohawk he's letting grow out hang ragged from the middle of his scalp. "How's it going?" Ambrose asks.

"Not as easy as I thought." Robert rubs his right shoulder, the spot where he's informed Ambrose he'll get his first tattoo when he turns eighteen.

"What is?" Ambrose asks. Robert nods, and Ambrose fidgets in the ensuing silence. "Can I borrow your laptop?" Ambrose holds up his camera. "I'm doing pictures with your grandmother."

"It's on my desk." Robert lies back down. The dolly wheels groan as he disappears beneath the car. "Plug it back in when you're done, okay?"

Ambrose closes the door and the grinder's wail diminishes as he walks away. In the basement area Robert's claimed for his room, Ambrose finds the computer amid the desk's clutter. Clothes piles crouch at the foot of his unmade bed. The crude cinderblock and wood-plank shelves are piled with paperbacks and CDs, the walls smothered with posters of skateboarders and punk bands. Ambrose lingers for a moment before exiting, laptop in hand.

At the dining room table, Ambrose sips iced tea and downloads pictures onto the laptop. Clementine arches against his shins. The shots, a parade of mundane images, flash across the screen, and beneath each, Ambrose types their names in bold, capital letters. The summer before second grade, his mother taped index cards throughout the rooms, neatly penned tags that betrayed her schoolteacher past. CUPBOARD. DRAWER. DESK. TABLE. Sometimes, out of the corner of his eye, Ambrose still sees a card, a trick of memory, a crossing of the internal circuits linking past and present.

He carries the laptop to the screened-in back porch where his mother sits, wearing a floral housedress and pink flip-flops. The scent of freshly cut grass flavors the warm breeze. In the garage, Robert has forsaken the grinder for a hammer. With each crunching blow, Ambrose flinches a bit, mourning the neighborhood's interrupted peace. The last clinging petals twist down from the cherry tree. A pink moat circles the trunk, a testament to Ambrose's unwillingness to disturb a scene so short-lived and unthinkably beautiful. *Petals,* he thinks. *Tree. Pink. Green.*

His mother's trembling fingers attempt to insert an earring. He guides her hand, and the post slides through a piercing made by her older sister the night Elvis debuted on Ed Sullivan. She hands him the other earring and turns her head. Ambrose smiles, imagining that long ago scene, the TV unplugged and the girl's tearful pleas ignored after their father discovered the holes in his daughter's earlobes.

Ambrose pulls up the first image, a still life of the piano that hasn't been played since his mother's stroke. Her doctors claim she's as healthy as can be expected, the possibility of another stroke tempered by her new regimen of pills. The cardiologist says her heart keeps a rhythm that puts his wristwatch to shame. The physical therapist works on her shaky hands but contends that her reflexes remain strong. The audiologist reports her hearing is fine. The neurologist points to a clean CAT scan that reveals no clouding of her cognitive centers. What the white-coated flock can't explain is her aphasia, the sudden and complete silence that's befallen her. She is complete in the sense that she feeds and bathes and dresses herself, yet without words, she often appears to Ambrose as if she's fading away, her edges blurred.

With a press of the spacebar, the letters that spell *piano* scroll across the picture's bottom. "Piano, Mother," Ambrose says. "Piano. Remember?"

Ambrose, the tail end of his workplace tie flung over his shoulder, labors over the stove. Water boils in a large pot and sausage sizzles in the frying pan. Ambrose checks his watch and slides garlic bread into the oven. Ambrose's mother shuffles in and pours herself a glass of water. She drinks, smiles at her son, then ambles toward the back porch.

"Mom?" Ambrose calls, but his only answer is the slam of the backdoor. Leaving the stove, he peers out the window, watching as she inspects the garden flowers. Sunlight glimmers on the blades of the scissors she pulls from her housedress pocket. Bending stiffly, she snips the stalks of the first blooming daylilies. "Robert?" Ambrose calls. "Could use a little help, son."

Ambrose washes the lettuce and arranges the leaves in a trio of salad bowls. His mother sits in the shade of the cherry tree, the cut lilies resting on her lap. Her age-spotted hands herd the petals into pink mounds. She's begun wandering this past week or two, drifting into their neighbors' yards, giving Ambrose a scare last Sunday at the supermarket. Ambrose studied her the other evening as she, letters in hand, passed the mailbox on their evening walk. "Mom?" he called, but she just lumbered ahead, not running off so much as heeding a voice she alone heard. Ambrose calls Robert again, but when the boy doesn't answer, Ambrose heads to the basement.

Robert sits before the computer, his headphones on. Again, Ambrose flicks the lights, not wanting to startle the boy. The whittled-down din of clanging metal comes from the headphones Robert removes, a violent assault countered by a syrupy Tennessee drawl. Since he started working on the car, Robert has scoured the Internet daily, downloading videos of construction and racing. He emails new friends in Arkansas and Ohio, Ontario and Wyoming, his inbox filled with exchanged tips and advice. At least he's not ogling porn, Ambrose thinks, allowing himself a smile. At least he's not cruising sites pushing hate or offering instructions on how to assemble a bomb with bathroom cleaning products. In this time of encroaching menace, at least he's made decent choices—with the exception of the knife incident, a weapon Robert claimed he'd brought as a last-ditch defense against the toughs he'd been trying to avoid since making the mistake of asking out one of their girlfriends.

"Need your help," Ambrose says. "Can you keep an eye on Grandma?"

The boy gathers his MP3 player and a set of earphones. Through the kitchen window, Ambrose watches his son help his mother rise from her cherry-petaled bed. The boy slows his pace, and they walk side-by-side. Ambrose's mother strikes a bride's pose, one hand grasping Robert's offered arm, the other clutching her lily bouquet. In the living room, Clementine rises from her sleeping perch atop the piano. Her padded feet play a spastic tune across the keys before she leaps down and joins the others in the dining room. Ambrose drains the pot, sweating in the unleashed current of steam. The microwave chirps. As Ambrose prepares their plates, he glances into the dining room where, to his surprise, his mother is wearing Robert's earphones.

"You're not making her listen to your music, are you?" Ambrose asks.

Robert slides the lilies into a vase and sets it on the dining room table. "I downloaded a bunch of songs from her time last night. Thought she'd get a kick out of them."

Ambrose brings their plates to the table, rising once, then again to retrieve the items he's forgotten—salad dressing, forks, the grated Parmesan his mother likes. When all is set, Robert gently removes his grandmother's earphones. For a moment, Ambrose pauses. What little faith he'd once had has abandoned him recently, yet sitting in his father's old chair, he feels an obligation to offer grace. He studies his folded hands. "Thank you, Lord, for our food and our family. Amen."

Robert shakes his shaggy head and picks up his fork. A hush settles over them, his mother's silence underpinned by the clatter of silverware, the barking of the neighbor's dog. As it has so often since his return home, the schism between what was and what is ambushes Ambrose, a realization whose dizzying implications are heightened by the perspective shift of Robert's claiming of Ambrose's old spot at the table. Instinctively, he reaches out and clasps his son's hand. Robert looks at his hand, then to Ambrose. He swallows his food. "You're freaking me out a little tonight, Dad."

Ambrose's mother grabs Ambrose's other hand and gives it a series of feeble squeezes. "Umm," she sputters, a guttural inflection realized at the base of her throat. Her normally placid eyes open wide as she frantically gestures over Robert's shoulder.

Ambrose turns to discover the kitchen shrouded in a black haze. Ambrose leaps to his feet, his chair clattering to the floor, his son close behind. A smoky torrent roils when Ambrose opens the oven door, the forgotten slabs of garlic bread charred rectangles. Using a dish towel, Ambrose retrieves the tray, dumps the smoldering chunks into the sink, and douses them with water. The smoke detector shrieks, and as Robert balances atop a chair and fumbles with the detector's battery, Ambrose's mother clamps her hands over her ears, an odd grin upon her lips.

Phone to his ear, Ambrose peeks over the top of his cubicle. There's the typical milling traffic, the coming and going of the water cooler and copy room. Liz, the-once-a-week plant lady, hums a vaguely familiar tune as she tends to the office's ferns and spider plants, the ficus tree that come Christmas will be strung with white lights. With his supervisor nowhere in sight, Ambrose sinks back into his chair, his vision field walled off once again.

A human voice interrupts the telephone's Muzak-bland whisper. Ambrose perks up, and in hushed, hurried tones, he relates his tale, the nightmare entanglements of insurance coverage for his mother. He opens the folder on his desk, shifting through the papers bearing preapprovals and evaluations and payments declined. The woman on the other line says, "Let me confer with my supervisor about that." Before Ambrose can beg her not to, she's placed him back on hold.

Ambrose sinks back into his chair. He swivels, surveying the walls of his cubicle, the calendar and dated Post-It notes, the memos and policy updates. Here is the bunker of modern life, a space whose only joy emanates from the framed picture of himself and Robert taken at the beach last summer. Ambrose rests a finger along the frame's edge, thinking of the snapshot only he knows remains nestled behind, a smiling photo of a slightly shorter Robert, his arms draped around the shoulders of Ambrose and Jill, his ex. How appropriate—this private haunting, her ghostly lingering behind the moment. He removes the frame's backing and slides out the photo. The morning Jill left, she packed her clothes and jewelry, took her morning grumpiness and goodnight kisses.

Ambrose, a cost analyst by trade and thus skilled in calculations and extrapolations, could have predicted these things, but when her loaded-down car pulled from the curb, what he couldn't have predicted was the greater absences that would find him, his life's unappreciated scaffolding of love and trust and faith sent crashing to the ground.

A woman's voice comes over the line, a brief question, and Ambrose is too disheartened to protest when he's exiled back to hold. These insurance people, his son, his mother, his co-workers, Ambrose feels as if they've adopted a new language, one whose words he understands but whose meanings and underlying emotions have turned slippery. He waits. And waits. Finally, he slumps forward, elbows on his desktop, and cradles his forehead in his hand.

"Hey there, Ambrose."

Ambrose stirs, momentarily fazed by the incongruity of the still-playing Muzak and the sound of his name.

"Up here." A woman's face, cut off beneath the nose, peers over the cubicle's top. The tan cap gives her away: Liz, the plant lady. "Sorry," she whispers. She cringes, using her water bottle to pantomime holding a phone to her ear.

"It's all right. I'm in limbo for the foreseeable future."

"Want a little Dieffenbachia?"

"Excuse me?"

"The one in the break room is growing like mad." She reaches over the cubicle's top and hands him a clear plastic cup lined with dirt and topped by broad, pale leaves. "It should survive here if you take care of it right. Spray it and set it near a window on the weekends."

Ambrose touches a leaf's pointed end. "You didn't mistakenly pick me out as a green-thumb type, did you?"

"I had you picked out as a guy who could use a little something living at his desk. Am I right or am I right?"

Ambrose sighs. "You're right."

"They're healthy. And it's good to have something real to look at once in a while."

He holds the plant to eye level. "Sure I can't kill it? I don't have the best track record with this kind of thing."

"Anything's possible, isn't it? I'll check in next week. I'll bring a spare pot if I remember. Until then, don't overwater it, okay?"

Pushing aside a marketing report he should have read yesterday, Ambrose clears a space for the plant. The Muzak stops, and Ambrose swivels in his chair, groping for his mother's file. "Hello? Hello?" he says, but the phone's red-light display has gone dark, its tiny gray monitor proclaiming, *Call Canceled*.

Alone on the living room couch, Ambrose's mother fiddles with Robert's MP3 player. Her head bobs slightly, a wispy, distant smile on her lips. Ambrose imagines the pretty teenage girl captured in the upstairs hallway pictures. He sees her brushing the long blond hair that would one day turn gray, Buddy Holly singing "That'll Be the Day" from the nightstand's tube-glowing radio. She removes an earphone and considers her son.

"I'm going jogging, Mom." Ambrose studies his ancient, grass-stained Nikes, the shorts that are actually his bathing trunks. In the new-found hush of their relationship, Ambrose finds himself uncharacteristically chatty, anxious to fill the silence with words. "Know I gave it up years ago, but I've been considering picking it up again. And a day this beautiful steals my excuses for putting it off until tomorrow." His mother smiles and replaces the earphone. Leaning close, he kisses her forehead.

Ambrose stretches in the backyard, a routine awkward and stiff, each new pose filtered through the hesitant questioning of memory. A squirrel picks through the shade of the cherry tree, the petals chopped and scattered by Ambrose's last lawn cutting. Robert's car, stripped of its muffler, revs in the garage, a perturbed, throaty roar. The racket chases the squirrel back into the cherry tree. Ambrose lifts his face to the sun, and for a moment, allows the warmth to sink beneath his skin.

He sets out. The first few minutes are surprisingly easy, the day's dry heat and the initial pulse-surge almost intoxicating, but by the fifth block, his elation wanes. His gait turns clumsy, his breathing labored. Complaints from his knees and hip hijack his notions of grace, and soon each stride feels like little more than a rescued fall. On he goes, willed by guilt and embarrassment, by the fading image of the man he wishes to be. Forward he plods, fueled by the disquieting news Robert shared last night over dinner—his belief that his mother may be in love with Mark, the man she's been seeing these past six months.

The lopsided gravity of the development's continually curving streets toys with his sense of balance. At the half-mile mark, he turns around, swallowing back the urge to walk. The street scenes of well-kept lawns and painted mailboxes blur, a low-grade, present-tense blindness in which his only clear vision is of his ex-wife. Jill has become the buoyant force in the swamp of his repressed consciousness, her memory refusing the watery grave he's tried so desperately to wish upon her. Up she rises, haunting his unguarded thoughts, a malevolent apparition in the silent and lonely moments of his life. Perhaps, Ambrose thinks, this grip is an equal and balancing force to the efforts he exerted to save their marriage during their final, painful months together. How he'd fought to keep her, the purchasing of inexpensive luxuries, the loving notes left on the kitchen counter. On the increasingly rare occasions she surrendered to his advances, she'd kiss him with an ebbing passion, finally reaching a point where she'd drift into a state of distraction, an almost childish lack of inhibitions that left her free to scratch her nose or adjust her hair. From these soul-bruising moments, Ambrose divined an unexpected, polar strain of emotion, his mathematician's desire to balance the equation between them leading to more passionate kisses, the whispering of the words he himself longed to hear.

Three more blocks, and the torment of his body has shrunk into something hard and jagged yet manageable, a pebble-in-the-shoe irritant compared to thoughts of Jill. He could forgive her for leaving him—Lord knows he was painfully aware of his own faults—but he couldn't forgive her for abandoning Robert, a boy as complicated as he is sensitive. When their paths cross at his weekend drop-offs or some meeting for school or court, Ambrose struggles to remain civil. He understands he can't blame her for the knife or the mohawk or the boy's increasingly morose attitude, yet he does. At first this rankling emotion perplexed him, the right-thinking mathematician stymied by the situation's irrationality, by its refusal to yield to an answer that was a sum of its parts. He'd never really hated another person, not for an extended period of time, but he can no longer deny his heart. He hates Jill.

Spurred by this unvented ire, he sprints the last block and a half. His chest swells and clenches. The street's black macadam moves beneath his numb feet, each exhalation marked by a pained grunt. He half stumbles onto his lawn, and once the momentum seeps from his legs, he bends forward and presses his hands into his knees. Sparks crisscross his vision field, and his ears swim with the thud of his agitated heart, a beat supported and reinforced by the metal-pounding racket echoing from his mother's garage.

Later that week, his knees still sore, Ambrose forsakes his jog for a twilight stroll. Back home, his mother listens to the latest songs Robert has downloaded. Robert sparks a welder's torch in the garage, a jittery glow like horror-movie lightning. Ambrose bids good evening to anonymous neighbors, admires gardens shading into bloom, stops an errant soccer ball from rolling into the street, and gently kicks it back to a waiting group of children. The fresh air and fading light calm the stubborn remnants of his day.

The streetlights shine down upon him as he returns to his block. All is quiet in the garage, and Ambrose smiles, happy that Robert has accepted his no-work-after-dark rule. Inside the foyer, he kicks off his shoes, another house rule, this one a survivor from his childhood when he'd return home with snow-clumped boots and muddy sneakers. His mother, absorbed in the sound woven by her headphones, doesn't glance up as he walks past.

Ambrose pours a glass of water then stands in the basement doorway. A garbled transmission plays from Robert's computer speakers. Ambrose calls his son's name, a greeting that also serves as a warning of his entrance. The laptop's monitor flickers with grainy footage, the chaotic scene gelling as Ambrose approaches. Robert says the video is from an Internet friend in Saskatchewan. Ambrose, sensing an opportunity to draw close to his often-distant son, pulls up a seat.

The screen light shimmers on their faces. Robert explains the basic rules and fundamental driving techniques. He points out the sandbaggers and the overly reckless, explains the roles of the officials who scamper amidst the smoking carnage. Finally, the checkered flag is raised over the battered and limping survivor. Robert retrieves another clip, and the odd spectacle intrigues Ambrose; the initial, prowling dance of crazily painted cars, a circling like blood-baited sharks around the tiny, earthen track. A green flag waves, and chaos descends upon the scene. Swirls of dust veil the hivelike swarming, a dirty scrim soon augmented by the smoky belches that escape the cars' crumpled hoods. Within five minutes, only two cars remain. Despite his initial reservations, Ambrose finds himself drawn to the action, thrilled in the same cringing manner with which he'll watch the last round of a heavyweight slugfest, the defenseless toe-to-toe exchanges that speak to a man's repressed, savage wiring. On the track, the tide turns again and again, retreats made not to escape but to garner a bit of momentum for the next attack. The cars lock in a spiraling, smoke-spewing embrace from which one emerges, the final assaults carried out in fitful, low-speed collisions upon a victim which can no longer move.

Ambrose watches two more derby videos before he bids his son goodnight. Upstairs, he showers, opens a beer, and retreats to his room. Propping his pillows behind him, he sits on the football-patterned bedspread his mother sewed for his ninth birthday. Unsettling sometimes, his waking in this cramped room, the shelves still lined with the books he read in junior high, the airplane models he glued on rainy Saturdays, the Little League trophy he once cherished even though he rarely took the field. How preserved and constant this space is, and Ambrose considers himself reintroduced into the scene, everything the same except for him, the setting's only fading and rotting element.

Ambrose sets his finished beer on the nightstand and retrieves the digital camera. He turns it on, his surroundings transplanted onto the back's tiny screen. With a button push, he accesses the memory card. His thumb upon the playback button, he clicks through the pictures he's taken for his mother—a chair, the refrigerator, the kitchen sink. Interspersed between these are shots of Robert's car, the documentation for his school: close-ups of stripped doors, the beneath-the-dash thicket of disconnected wires, the tangle of glass and plastic waiting to be hauled to the junkyard. When he bought the camera, Ambrose opted for the largest memory card available. Now he finds himself drifting back to predivorce images, shots of Jill and himself and Robert on a sandy beach, Jill in a sun hat posing in a palm tree's shade, Ambrose with his arm around his son. He stops at a close-up of himself and Jill. He aches to shout to his old self, the oblivious dupe who didn't see that times had changed, who couldn't comprehend the crushing weight of misplaced love that was at that very moment barreling toward his blind side.

His eyes grow heavy. He turns out the light. Tomorrow's workday looms, deadlines and obligations and meetings that require his firm planting in the here and now, but for the moment, he keeps his thumb planted on the camera's image-shuffling button. One by one, the brightly lit images fly past, achieving a herky-jerky unity, a disjointed movie that, in its own unconscious manner, tells a story familiar yet impossible to truly understand.

Ambrose spreads a section of the rain-dampened Sunday paper across the kitchen table. Robert, his eyes puffy with sleep, finally emerges from his room. Cereal bowl in hand, he grunts "Good morning," claims the seat opposite Ambrose, and begins to shovel milk-dripping spoonfuls to his mouth. Robert's work on the car has reached a temporary impasse, the boy disappointed because a part he ordered won't arrive until Tuesday. Ambrose considers the day ahead—the sluggish pace born of gray skies and long silences and afternoon naps—and, turning another damp-edged page, he comes up with the idea of taking in a matinee, the deal sweetened by an offer to let Robert drive. Together, they discuss the films playing at the local cineplexes, weeding through the teen sex comedies and shoot-'em-up thrillers until they select a slice-of-life art film showing at the Savoy, the old, single-screen theater downtown.

On the ride, Ambrose revisits the uneasiness of the passenger seat, a tight-lipped apprehension similar to the way he once felt jogging beside Robert on his first two-wheeler spins. The rain falls harder and the wipers slap a nervous beat. When Robert was a boy, Ambrose could reach out and steady his path, could catch him before he fell, but like so much else now, his ability to step in and make things right has diminished. Ambrose holds his tongue at Robert's indecision at four-way stops, cringes at the boy's hydroplaning pedal stomps. In the backseat, Ambrose's mother switches tracks on Robert's MP3 player.

Robert parks the car, and the three of them cross the puddled lot. Ambrose's mother, flanked by her son and grandson, dictates their dawdling pace, her gray head kept dry by the increasingly soggy classifieds section Ambrose and Robert hold above her. In the theater's lobby, Ambrose's wet skin erupts in gooseflesh beneath the air conditioner's chill. Robert balls up the dripping newspaper and stuffs it in a nearby trashcan. Ambrose has always loved the Savoy, its Art Deco sensibilities and the memories it holds, the movies he's seen here with his mother and father, the nervous teen dates. He absently hands his money to the cashier, his attention drawn to his mother, who's migrated to the candy counter. He grabs his tickets and is about to walk off when he hears his name.

"Ambrose?" the voice repeats.

Taken back, Ambrose glances across the counter to discover Liz, the office's plant lady. "This is a surprise."

"How's that Dieffenbachia?" she asks.

"Surviving if not exactly thriving. But I have the best of intentions to replant it soon. And you're right; it is nice to have something green at my desk."

"Only makes sense, doesn't it?" Liz steps aside and gestures to the teenage girl behind her. "Ambrose, this is my daughter Emilia."

The girl glances up from the paperback book cradled in her lap. A curtain of straight black hair hangs down over one eye, and with a deft finger-sweep, she tucks it behind a thrice-pierced ear. A black Ramones T-shirt drapes her lanky torso. She mutters a barely audible hello and returns to her book.

Ambrose rests his hand on his son's shoulder. "This is Robert. He may or may not admit to being my son, depending on his mood."

Robert shrugs off his father's hand. "Very funny, Dad." He nods to Liz and Emilia. "Nice to meet you."

"And over there is my mother. Would you like to fetch her, Robert?"

Robert lopes across the lobby and joins her at the candy counter. Emilia sighs and sets down her book. "Should I see what they want?" she asks.

"That's what you're getting paid for," Liz says.

Emilia slides off her stool and offers a lazy salute. "Yes, sir."

"Didn't know you worked here." Ambrose steps aside as Liz sells tickets to an elderly couple.

"Plants and movies. Two of my favorite things. I'm a licensed projectionist." She closes the register drawer. "How old is your boy?"

"Seventeen. And Emilia?"

"Sixteen." Liz smiles. "Sixteen and she never tires of letting me know how ridiculous I am."

"I hear they come around eventually," Ambrose says.

Their smiles ebb into a hesitant silence. "I'd better get to the booth," Liz says.

They exchange goodbyes. Robert leads the way to the theater, the carpet worn and faded by the years. When the lights go down, Ambrose gazes back to the trio of lit rectangular windows cut into the back wall. The raspy cadence of his mother's breathing hums in the darkness, and in an underlying whisper, he detects the muffled strains from her still-playing earphones, a couplet of quiet tones swiftly engulfed by the blaring volume of movie trailers. The feature starts, and Ambrose's eyes, now adjusted to the dark, gaze over the theater, a sea of empty seats dotted by clumps of singletons and pairs. Ambrose enjoys the movie's first half hour, the pretty faces and the absorption into a fictional world where the problems aren't his own. Robert fidgets a bit, the narrative's sluggish pace no doubt of little interest to a teen who dreams of the demolition derby. Just as the leads yield to temptation and kiss, his mother leans over and hands the earphones and MP3 player to Robert. She stands and plods slowly up the sloped aisle. Robert holds one of the plugs to his ear, his thumb testing the player's buttons. "Charge is gone," he whispers.

Ambrose follows his mother. In the lobby, blinking beneath the sudden light, she parks herself in front of the candy counter and points to a box of lemon drops. "No charge," Liz says when Ambrose opens his wallet. His mother plucks a piece into her mouth, and her lips contort into a puckered smile.

Emilia, sitting on her stool behind the counter, turns another page in her book. Ambrose's mother pops two more lemon drops and winces happily. Robert appears. "Were you going to leave me in there all alone? That movie really sucks."

"Tell me about it," Emilia says before Ambrose can correct his son.

"I've got to change the reel." Liz gestures to a shut door behind the counter. "Want to check out the booth? It's where all the magic happens."

"Just like Disneyland," Emilia says unenthusiastically.

With Liz in the lead and Emilia bringing up the rear, the five of them climb single-file up the narrow stairwell and through a door labeled "Employees Only." A muted light shines inside. The projector's unrelenting purr reminds Ambrose of a woodland stream. Bending over, he picks up a two-inch snippet of film. Emilia lifts the next reel from the strap-laced container and secures it to the second projector. Liz tugs the film's end and laces it through the machine's labyrinth of cogs and rollers. Ambrose, excusing himself as he maneuvers the cramped space never intended for five, stands before the cutout window between the projectors. The projector's beam knifes into the darkness, suffuses and becomes lost in the theater's empty space before its glorious resurrection on the screen. Ambrose rubs the strip of film between his fingers, his thumb tracing the sprocket holes. A whispered timing click signals the switch from one projector to the other, not a beat skipped upon the screen. Ambrose's mother nudges her son aside and gazes through the window's opening.

"Robert, would you like a soda?" Liz asks. She raises the first projector's take-up arm and loops the tail end around the front's empty reel. With a flick, the reels spin. The trail of film hisses softly.

"Sure," Robert says. "Thanks."

"Go with Robert, Emilia," Liz says. "It will give you two a chance to compare notes about the weirdness of your parents."

"Like it's not painfully obvious." Emilia blushes. "I mean yours is, not Robert's dad's."

"Just give him a few minutes," Robert says. "He won't let you down."

They leave, and for the next reel, Ambrose, his mother, and Liz remain in the booth. Ambrose's mother maintains her post by the window as she finishes off the lemon drops. Ambrose and Liz speak in hushed voices of plants and movies and of the trials of raising a pair of teenagers they love more than life itself.

The playground of Ambrose's youth still occupies a grassy lot a few blocks from his mother's house. The space has been revamped, the seesaws and merry-go-round removed for fear of lawsuits, and in their place, plastic slides and harnessed swings, a patch of rubber matting beneath the jungle gym.

Ambrose sweats in his parked car in the playground's lot. He shifts his cell phone to his other hand and loosens his tie. The afternoon sun blazes, a miragelike glare on the deserted landscape of plastic and metal. Almost gone, his recollections of climbing and swinging, and this sense of kidnapped time even spills into adulthood. He now has trouble clearly remembering bringing Robert here, the details slipping away until all he retains is the memory of Robert's sweaty, clasping hand, the boy's body pogoing with excitement as they neared the sandbox and slide.

"Ambrose, are you listening to me?"

"I pulled over so I could listen all the better, Jill."

"I know you. You're off in thought while we're trying to iron this out."

"You're angry again." Ambrose sighs. "What else do I need to know? You're angry and soon I will be too if I listen close enough."

She grunts. "You're infuriating."

"Robert wants to stay here this weekend, Jill. Trust me. And if you don't, then call him, but I'd rather save him from all the drama."

"Do you really think I'd involve him like that or in any way that would hurt him?"

Ambrose chokes back the urge to bring up Mark. "No, I don't." A man and his leashed dog walk past. "And he doesn't want to be with me, if that's any consolation. He just wants to work on the car."

Ambrose tells her the latest about the car. Jill laughs and asks if Ambrose remembers the time Robert, no more than seven, took apart her mother's ancient alarm clock, its cogs and springs and coils spread like shrapnel across the living room floor. "Yes," Ambrose says, "I remember." Silence, and then they get on with the task of switching a weekend next month. The arranging of calendars, the chilled exchanges of money, a brief, shared memory of their only child—here are the surviving intersections of their once-joined lives. Her voice still bears the sting of it all, and Ambrose despises himself for the knee-jerk cattiness he initiates, for the innuendoes he hurls for no other reason than to mask his wounded pride. Ambrose closes his eyes as Jill goes on about the colleges Robert should visit before summer ends. He wishes he could surrender, wishes he could release the anger that only roots him in the hurtful past, but he can't. He just can't.

Five minutes later, he pulls into his mother's driveway. The garage door is open, and the shadowed space inside is dominated by Robert's soon-to-be-destroyed car. Robert leans beneath the raised hood. Grocery bag in hand, Ambrose steps into the garage, taken aback to see Robert has company. There is Emilia, bathed in the queer light shed from a caged bulb hung from the hood's underside. Perched atop an overturned bucket, she glances up from her lap-balanced sketchbook and waves to Ambrose.

"Nice to see you, Emilia." He's cautiously elated, happy that Robert—so often a content if somewhat sullen loner—has made a new friend. He considers the girl and his son, thinking of how few teenagers seem comfortable in their skin, preferring to recede behind a scrim of manners or eye-obscuring bangs or a floor-locked gaze.

Robert stands, wipes his hands on a rag, and introduces his father to the older boy examining the engine from the other side of the car. "This is Rick. He's Daryl's older brother."

Ambrose extends a hand, but Rick, grinning widely, holds up his grease-slathered palms. Ambrose faintly remembers Rick, an older sibling from Robert's playground days, a rambunctious child and jungle-gym daredevil, a boy whose father once confessed to Ambrose that every night when the phone rang, both he and his wife cringed, fearing another call from one of Rick's teachers. Rick, now a community college dropout and a two-year veteran of the county fair's demolition derby, has taken up Robert's offer to be his driver.

Robert lowers the light deep into the engine's guts. The young men lean closer, their faces eerily illuminated in the shine, their looming shadows projected onto the walls and ceiling. As the boys discuss rewiring the ignition, Emilia pages through her sketchbook, showing Ambrose the designs she's considering for the car's paint job. "What do you like better for the trunk?" she asks, flipping between a sketch of a round, fuse-lit bomb and a billowing mushroom cloud.

Rick excuses himself, citing his boss' threats to fire him if he's late again. He raises a fist, and he and Robert tap knuckles then lightly bump chests. Ambrose imagines Robert's eye-popping disgust if his father decided to replicate the ritual's tap-thump instead of offering Rick a simple wave. Handshakes and hairstyles, fashion and incomprehensible lingo—they are the domain of the young, and no amount of posturing could lend authenticity to a generational interloper struggling to stay hip. Only natural, Ambrose thinks, youth's desire to define itself, to glom onto the customs unique to the living, breathing present. His time in those years has passed, and he could no more reclaim his right to such rituals than he could make Jill love him again.

Rick's rusted pickup rumbles from the curb. "So he's your man?" Ambrose asks.

Robert tweaks the radio's volume and turns his attention back to the engine. "Yep."

Ambrose addresses Emilia. "And what's planned for the hood?"

"I'm debating whether or not to keep the bomb thing going."

"A motif perhaps?" Ambrose asks.

She shrugs. "I guess."

Robert, still bent over the front quarter-panel, offers Ambrose an annoyed look that could have been grafted off his mother's face.

"I'd better get dinner started." Ambrose pauses. "Emilia, would you like to join us?"

"Sure. Cool," she says. Robert, wrench in hand, doesn't look up.

Ambrose shuts the garage door behind him. He lingers for a moment on the other side, eavesdropping on a conversation yet to begin. He smiles at the silence, smiles at the thought of Robert and Emilia, the two of them rich in gifts they're powerless to appreciate, more innocent than they would ever acknowledge or comprehend.

Ambrose's four-cylinder compact weaves aggressively through the midafternoon traffic. His destination—the hospital emergency room, the workday drudgery of his cubicle shattered by a nurse's call. Ambrose pressed, but the nurse, citing privacy laws, only provided the sketchiest of details of Robert's condition and instead urged Ambrose to come to the hospital immediately and speak to a doctor. Ambrose halts, looks both ways, then runs a red light, the race rejoined. His cell rings, but the incoming number is unfamiliar, so he lets it take a message. Playing in his head are the chilling scenarios of teen tragedy—car accidents and overdoses, suicide attempts—and the whirling images only make his foot press heavier on the gas. Angry horns bleat in his wake.

Finding no spaces in the lot's first two rows, Ambrose parks on a grassy patch near the emergency room doors. He bounds out, and as he nears the shaded sidewalk beneath the entrance's overhang, he spots Liz, a cell phone to her ear and a puzzled look on her face. She closes her phone. "I was just trying to call you again."

The entrance's automatic doors sigh open, and as they step into the lobby, Liz hurriedly recounts Emilia's tale of Robert's fall from their garage roof: the boy stopping over to borrow some CDs, Emilia's offer to share a lemonade at the backyard picnic table before he biked home, the neighborhood brothers who'd thrown their Frisbee onto Liz's garage roof. Robert had no trouble retrieving the Frisbee, the boys cheering, Emilia applauding her hero, but Robert fumbled in his attempt to step back onto the ladder. His plummet landed inches from the driveway's concrete— thank God—but Emilia said even with the grassy cushion, she heard the snap of his wrist, the hand he'd reflexively held out to break his fall buckling queasily beneath his weight.

"I should have called you right away," Liz says, "but when I saw him, I could only think about getting him here. He was really brave. You'd have been proud." Emilia joins them at the triage desk, hovering behind her mother and nibbling her fingernails. "When Robert gave your name to the nurse, it finally hit me that I still needed to call you, but I wanted to stay with him until they were done admitting him. And by then, I couldn't get through."

"Exam area three," the desk nurse says, pointing to a set of doors at the end of a short hallway.

Liz follows him for a few steps then halts. "I'll let you see him alone."

Ambrose stops and turns. "Thanks. I should have said that before. Thanks. Both of you."

"You're welcome," Liz says. "And Ambrose? Your wife's back there, too."

Ambrose pushes through the swinging doors. His head swirls, the adrenaline flood that had seized him subsiding, an emotional vacuum swiftly claimed by a jagged, almost tearful brand of relief. And now, on top of it all, Jill. He peeks between the gaps left by hanging curtains not fully drawn, fleeting scenes of distress and bloody bandages. Finally he reaches the one that offers a sliver of his son's black shirt and telltale haircut.

Jill and Robert glance up when Anbrose pushes the curtain aside. A white-smocked doctor stands before Robert, his attention focused on Robert's hand which he tenderly grasps by the wrist. Robert winces. Unshed tears ring his eyes. "Sorry, Dad."

"Liz said it was some fall." Ambrose stands on the other side of the examination table from Jill. He offers a forced smile over their son's bowed head. Her hair has changed since he saw her two weeks ago, shorter and blonder, more businesslike.

"Well, mom and dad," the doctor says, "my guess is Robert has a broken wrist. But before we do an X-ray and get a cast on it, we need to attend to these fingers."

For the first time, Ambrose studies his son's hand. The flesh is red and swollen from the middle of the forearm down. With one hand, the doctor pinches Robert's palm, and with the other, he turns his attention to the three fingers—index, middle, and ring—each horribly bent at the middle knuckle. "When I slide it back in, it will really sting for a moment," the doctor says. "Ready, son?"

Robert nods. Ambrose lays a hand on his son's shoulder. The doctor clamps onto the tip of Robert's index finger and delivers a swift tug. The sickening *pop* radiates into Ambrose's hand, and he reflexively clutches Robert's shoulder. "Crap!" Robert spits.

Ambrose bites his lip. A young man wishes for the worldly gifts of adventure and love and irresponsible freedom; a father, older and supposedly wiser, only wishes for the impossible burden of assuming his children's pain. Robert grunts after the second, queasy *pop*.

Robert sucks a deep breath through clenched teeth. Ambrose rubs his son's softly heaving back, and at the nub of the boy's spine, his hand collides with Jill's. They consider each other over Robert's bowed head. Here, he thinks, is a bond stronger than the smoking wreckage of their life together. In whatever alignment the fates allow, here remains the niche the three of them have carved from an indifferent world, a space he desires to fill only with his best self. In this moment of anguish and relief, he forgives her, spontaneously and without thought, forgives her for their son and for himself and for the future they all must live, and as he does, a weight he'd barely been conscious of abandons him. The spasm that accompanies the next realigned finger triggers a final shudder in Robert's body, and when the doctor is done, both father and son pause to wipe tears from their eyes.

A few hours later, Ambrose, Liz, Robert, and Emilia stop at a bookstore on the ride home. Painkillers have turned Robert mellow and agreeable, his typical blasé attitude replaced with a lazy jolliness. A cast runs from his knuckles to the meat of his forearm, the snowy plaster coated with a blue wrap that now bares the glitter-pen signatures of his father, Liz, and Emilia. Ambrose and Liz claim a table in the store's coffee shop. Emilia and Robert wander to the music section. Every so often, Ambrose catches a glimpse of Emilia tiptoeing up to place a set of headphones over Robert's ears. Steam hisses from the espresso machine and late afternoon sunshine streams through the windows. Liz and Ambrose laugh about their children and themselves, and for a change, Ambrose's thoughts, unhaunted by the ghost of his wife or betrayals, reside firmly in the present, a moment made richer by sunshine and the steamy aroma of just-brewed coffee, by a bit of shared laughter and a wellspring of thankfulness.

During the three weeks between Robert's accident and the demolition derby, Ambrose helps his son put the finishing touches on the car. Together, they chain the engine to the motor mounts, insulate the spark plug and ignition wires with sections of old hose and duct tape. They help Emilia with the artwork's final touches—the hood's roiling mushroom cloud, the door's number—*1023*—Robert's birthday, the quarter-panel ads for the junkyard and trash-hauling service which Robert has bartered for trade.

In the cricket-chirping evenings of late summer after his mother has gone to sleep, Ambrose often joins Robert in the basement where they watch derby videos, Ambrose picking up both the lingo and an appreciation for the sport's violent aesthetic. Other nights, Emilia joins them, bringing her DVDs of classic samurai and horror films. Ambrose watches a scene or two, wary of overstaying his welcome before bidding them goodnight. On the way to his teenage room, he sometimes opens the garage door off the laundry room and flicks the light. The car sits in the closed space stinking of oil and paint, its stripped form and bomb-blasting scenes a comical ode to the apocalypse, to a giddy, senseless anarchy that makes about as much sense as anything else in Ambrose's muddled days.

On the afternoon of the derby, Liz backs her brother's SUV into the driveway. Robert has borrowed a tow bar from the junkyard dealer, and Ambrose and Liz hook it to the trailer hitch, then to the car. When they're done, Ambrose steps back and, after studying the securing chains, questions the setup's legality. "I think we're okay," Liz says, wiping her hands on a rag. "It would take a real prick of a cop to ticket a car heading to its final ride."

Robert tries to call Rick, but after getting no answer, he announces they should be going and that Rick is probably already at the fairgrounds. Ambrose claims the SUV's passenger seat, Robert and Emilia flanking Ambrose's mother in the back. Liz dons her sunglasses, offers Ambrose a conspirator's smile, and eases into the street. They have grown closer these past weeks, lingering to chat when one drops off their child at the other's house, exchanging books, a Saturday afternoon spent at the local flea market. Liz has brought over Crock-Pot soups, and Ambrose has watched movies from the theater's projector booth.

Ambrose considers the car's shimmying rear end in the passenger-side mirror. In the backseat, Emilia and Ambrose's mother share the MP3 player's earplugs, while Robert tries to reach Rick again. Twenty minutes later, they enter the fairgrounds. The SUV trundles over the rutted earth and tire-matted grass, and their pitches and lurches resurrect Ambrose's tow-bar anxieties. With a security guard's wave, they're granted access through the grandstand's gate. Robert points the way to the pit, and Ambrose works up a sweat as he helps his son unhook the car. Ambrose pulls out his camera and snaps a series of pictures. Robert posing beside the car. Robert and Emilia perched atop the mushroom-clouded hood. Robert and his grandmother. The five of them in a shot taken by a fellow driver. The final shot is Robert and one of the derby judges exchanging a left-handed shake before the judge's inspection.

The setting sun peeks above the grandstand's press box. Ambrose's mother wanders toward the midway, and Ambrose and Liz bid their children goodbye, promising they'll be back in time for the race. At the picnic pavilion's communal benches, they eat sausage sandwiches and onion rings. Evening shadows bathe the fairgrounds in a hazy gray, and on Ambrose's arms, the slight chill hints of autumn's approach. Grease-flecked smoke rises from the sausage stand's open grill, and about twenty feet up, it catches the last sunlight rays before disappearing. In the budding darkness, Ambrose and Liz exchange stories about prom dates and honeymoons and the trips they'd like to take before they die.

Ambrose wipes sauce from his mother's chin before the three of them rejoin the bustling crowd. It's darker now, and the barkers begin their competing calls; Ambrose smiles, thinking of them as

forest birds, each given their own unique song. Sagging strings of
white lights line the midway. Calves and goats and llamas stroll in
hay-lined pens. Metallic, clattering notes emanate from the Octopus
and Ferris wheel and a half dozen other rides of dubious
construction. The fueling currents of the rides and lights seem to
have divined their way into the scampering packs of children whose
piping voices and squeaking sneakers provide the midway with a
nervously ecstatic undertow. Felled bottles clang at the baseball
toss, wheels of chance spit out their machine-gun rhythms, and
every so often, a young girl passes carrying a stuffed animal as
wonderful as it is ridiculous.

Ambrose allows his mother to take the lead. In the unclaimed
patches between the midway's booths and rides, she is reduced to
a silhouette, a black form haloed by the carnival's glow. Ambrose,
observing the shuffling distance between himself and his mother,
reaches out and holds Liz's hand. His heart, so heavy this past
year, swells a bit when she offers a reassuring squeeze.

Garbled rock music plays over the grandstand's speakers. The
bleachers hum with activity, men carrying drinks and cardboard
trays of hot dogs and nachos filing in to claim their seats, women
struggling to reign in their cranky and sunburned children. In the
pits, engines rev and men shout to be heard about the roar, the
final checks made before hoods are slammed in exclamation, but
when Ambrose finds Robert, his car is silent. His son and Emilia
perch dejectedly on the hood. Robert taps his cast against the
mushroom cloud. "Rick's not coming. He's in jail. Something about
a bar fight last night."

A megaphone to his mouth, a race official walks past. "All drivers
report to the judges' stand for final instructions. Five minutes until
the final instructions meeting at the judges' stand."

Ambrose's mother runs a finger along the front quarter-panel.
In the throaty decrescendo of engines shutting down, Ambrose
considers his son. Gone are their bike-riding days when a touch of
the hand could right the boy's path. Gone are the nightmare
awakenings Ambrose soothed with a kiss and a hug. The fairgrounds'

bristling din recedes, and the silence that descends upon Ambrose weighs heavy with words unspoken and answers not given. Robert hangs his head and slouches into the same defeated pose he assumed the day Ambrose arrived at school to find him handcuffed in the principal's office, the same he wore the night his mother backed her packed-to-bursting car out of the driveway. "I'll drive," Ambrose says to Robert. "If you'll have me."

Before Ambrose can balance the equations of costs and benefits, he finds himself at the judges' table signing a host of release forms. Liz smiles between lip-nibbling expressions of concern. Emilia is almost giddy as she hands Ambrose a white crash helmet. Ambrose studies the amorphous Rorschach design on one side. "It's a skull and crossbones," Emilia explains. She turns the helmet over. "This side's better, don't you think?" Ambrose tries on the helmet. His mother stares unabashedly.

Ambrose reassures Robert on the way to the drivers' meeting. "I've seen enough videos to be more than a complete novice, right?" he asks. Together, they rehash the basics. No sandbagging. No hits to the driver's side. Use the back end when possible. Avoid the track's center. Steer away from collisions. At the judges' table, Ambrose studies the drivers, young men half his age, their hands callused, many with cheeks balled with chewing-tobacco wads.

Back in the pit, he slides on a pair of safety glasses and adjusts the helmet's chin strap. Emilia snaps his picture, and Ambrose's eyes swim for a moment in the flash's echo. Robert winces when Ambrose attempts to open the welded-shut driver's door. With the help of his son and Liz, Ambrose awkwardly wedges himself through the window. Liz leans close. "I could almost mistake you for Steve McQueen."

Ambrose buckles up. The five-point harness makes him feel as though he's readying himself to jump from a plane. "Tell me I'm doing the right thing."

"You're doing the right thing, Ambrose." She gives his cheek a kiss. "The smart thing? That's another matter."

"At least you know the way to the hospital."

"At least."

The engine roars, and the solid vibration invades Ambrose's bones. Robert leans into the car and secures the keys in the ignition with a duct tape strip. He pauses. "Sure you want to do this, Dad?"

"You're the one who told me this is safe." Ambrose holds up his fist, and Robert surrenders a smile as they tap knuckles.

"It's safe for people who know what they're doing, Dad."

The other cars begin to move, a single-file, dirt-swirling caravan out of the pit's gate and onto the track. "Your old man's a quick learner. In some things at least. And think of the story we'll both have to tell when it's all over."

A judge waves Ambrose to join the line's end. Ambrose shifts into drive, but when he goes to check the missing rearview mirror, he only sees a slice of the summer night sky. With a gas-pedal nudge, the car rumbles forward. Dirt and fumes drift through the glassless windshield. He follows the others into the track's glaring spotlight shine. His pulse spikes as the cars perform their sultry prowl around the track. He studies his competitors, a black car adorned with red devils, a gray beast dubbed *The Widow Maker*. An indistinct voice calls over the loudspeaker, and the crowd cheers. Standing atop the hood of a monstrous pickup, one of the judges raises the green flag.

Ambrose catches a glimpse of his mother, Robert, Emilia, and Liz in the pit. With his left hand extended out the window, he offers them a wave. He's laughing, nervous for sure, but also tickled by the lovely absurdity of the moment. All sense of fear leaves him. The flag drops, and Ambrose tromps the gas, his eyes opened wide as he joins the fray.

A Different War

S now covered the football field, a white blanket for the sideline
markers and long pine benches. Impossible now to imagine
the jammed bleachers bristling with pennants, the cheerleaders'
shoes kicking up cinder clouds. Gloved fingers twining the chain
link fence, George Kates stared over the field, unable to see the
far goalpost through the fog. Nearer, the gym lights shimmered
across the snow, and although George had never seen the ocean,
he imagined this was how the moon might look on the endless
water. He walked toward the school, his boots crunching over the
snow's hardened crust, and stopped when the light touched his
pants. Inside the gym, the Tuesday night wrestling match was
starting. The crowd's muffled roar reached into the fog. The din
grew, a cry for victory. For blood.

Anna's father had drowned, his boat torpedoed, her mother
working twelve-hour shifts on the Philadelphia docks. Now Anna
was moving to their little town to live with Miss Dello, her aunt
and George's next door neighbor. When Anna stepped out of her
aunt's car and stood beneath the streetlight's cone of white, George
and his father hurried out to carry her trunk. The wind snared
Anna's long black hair, twisted the hem of her coat. Inside, she
waited at the top of the stairs. The hall light shone behind her, the
silhouette of her thin legs visible through her white dress. Shadows
obscured her face, yet her smell was distinct, a mix of perfumed

powder and train station rest rooms, cigars and coal smoke, soap for her neck and face. When George took a quicker step toward her, the trunk's handle ripped from his father's grasp and crashed onto the stairs.

George's fist connected with Vincent Sawyer's chin, a blow so square and solid that the bone-on-bone shock rode into George's shoulder. Vincent staggered back, tromping his crude portrait of a woman with baseball-sized breasts and a bushy triangle between her legs. Beneath the drawing, the name ANNA in capital letters. The other boys whistled, stomped their feet, a racket amplified by the tile and porcelain of the boys' basement lav, a clamor so driving and violent George became lost within it. Vincent tried to fight back, but the few punches that connected hurt George less than a slap from his mother. A shot to the ribs plastered Vincent against the wall, and his disheveled hair fanned out against a poster that urged *SAVE! SERVE! CONSERVE!* George latched onto Vincent's collar. He threw a punch for the other boys who'd laughed at the drawing. A punch for Anna and another for her father. A punch because he'd dropped her trunk like an oaf. A punch for the way he followed her in the hall so he could smell the air she'd just passed through.

   Knees bending in different directions, Vincent slumped to the floor. The trickling blood from his nose spotted his shirt. George's still-clenched fists weighed like hammers at his sides, his chest heaving the way it did when he ran wind sprints. He loomed over Vincent, praying the jerk would get up so he could pummel him all over again, but Vincent showed no interest in continuing the fight. The rage in George deflated with each breath flavored by the turpentine and sawdust drifting from the woodshop across the hall. He'd been wondering if he could kill a man, and now he trembled with a sudden knowledge that left him both fearful and relieved. He scooped up the drawing, stuffed it in his shirt pocket, and stormed out the door.

Friday night at the Bijou. First came George Burns and Gracie

Allen hawking war bonds. A Bugs Bunny cartoon. Coming
attractions and a reminder for ladies to please remove their hats.
The sports news was next, and baseball's top rookie raised his
pitching arm as he was sworn into the Marines. A Florida horse
race. Sonja Henie. Then the latest from the war. Hundreds of
soldiers in helmets and backpacks climbed a rickety gangplank.
George touched his head, and imagined a helmet's crowning
weight. He nudged closer, feeling the warmth of Anna's shoulder
against his. She didn't pull away.

A stable fire at the farm just outside George's end of town. George
and his father and the other neighborhood men sprinted across
the alfalfa field's rutted earth, the snow kicked up in clumps from
their boots, but they arrived too late to save the animals. The fire
crackled, and the neighing of trapped beasts disturbed George in
a way he couldn't have predicted. Gritty clouds wafted over him,
and George, holding a hand over his mouth, thought perhaps this
was the smell of war—the ashy-dry odor of burning wood, the
tangy stench of charred meat. It was the flavor of things never
meant to last, the flavor of passing trains and the gunpowder
residue that lingered after the last Fourth of July firecracker had
exploded. It was a flavor unlike baking bread or foundry smoke,
smells that promised a result a man could cradle in his hands. The
air around him now held a dwindling smell that promised nothing
except there would soon be less instead of more.

George and Anna crossed the rocky shore, the quarry turned to ice
as far as he could see, a dusty mirror for the clouds. The pines
surrounding the quarry stood still, and their green branches bowed
beneath the deep winter snow. He led her away from the busy section
of the ice where parents glided along slowly beside their bundled
children. A bit farther out, a pack of boys played hockey with an
empty can. The boys chased the rattling tin, their homemade sticks
whapping the ice. George and Anna climbed over a spill of boulders.
The footing on the boulders proved uneven, the clinging snow biting

through his gloves, the shaded nooks between the cracks coated with black ice. The skates Anna had slung over her shoulder swayed as she climbed. For a moment, George stood atop the slippery peak and looked back at the woods, the hockey players, the stumbling children. On the ice nearest him, Ricky Hughes glided past with his sad-eyed sweetheart. Last year, Ricky had been captain of the school's baseball team; next weekend he'd be shipping off to boot camp, leaving home with nothing but a toothbrush, razor, and the clothes on his back. Cheek to cheek, Ricky and his girl skated, balanced atop a world George's science teacher promised would never stop spinning. George thought about how things had changed during the war, Anna moving in with her aunt, Ricky and the dozens like him who'd kissed their families goodbye and boarded outbound trains. It was as if one end of the earth had been lifted, shaking people loose from their old lives, and away they went, bouncing like silver balls in a carnival sideshow game, some coming to rest far from where they'd started, some disappearing forever.

When George and Anna snuck into George's garage, they never pulled the light cord. One hand reaching back for Anna's, the other groping through a darkness haunted by fumes of paint and oil, George led Anna to the two crates he'd set in the floor's only clearing. When they kissed, George forgot about the war and the claims so many had upon him, his only concerns the soft push of her lips and the heady taste of her breath mingling with his.

Spring came, and the orderly rows of green sprouted in the alfalfa field. Red *X*'s ticked off the first days of May on Mrs. Neider's classroom calendar, less than six weeks to graduation. In P.E. class, Coach Davis had abandoned baseball and track and replaced them with endless marching drills. In their gym shorts and T-shirts, the senior boys paraded around the unlined football field, baseball bats and brooms and field hockey sticks slung over their shoulders. Watching the fumble-stepped drills, George made a silent list of the ways a soldier could die. Getting shot in the head or ripped open by a bomb—at least they'd be quick. As Mrs. Neider diagrammed another sentence on the board, George held his breath and counted to twenty, figuring that was how long it would take a plane to plummet from the sky. But he decided what he feared most was drowning or being burnt, his corpse sunk to the ocean floor or charred to a bony dust, all traces of his life erased, as if he'd never existed at all.

The cups were filled to their rims, and the red punch sloshed over George's fingers. Stepping carefully, he crossed the gymnasium floor, avoiding the snaking electrical cords that led to blue and red stage lights set on clunky tripods. Streamers dangled from the ceiling, the paper strips wavering in an otherwise imperceptible breeze. Moonlight washed the caged windows above the bleachers. The wrestling mats, rolled into thick cylinders, had been pushed against a far wall.

Anna sat alone at the foot of the bleachers. Mesh-patterned moonglow lit the white gardenia tucked behind her ear. Punch spilled onto her fingers as she took the cup.

The band eased into a slow song. George handed her a napkin. "You want to dance?"

She smiled. "That's what we came for, isn't it?"

Counting under his breath, George navigated the crowded floor near the stage. Nearby, Principal Williams danced with Mrs. Neider, his metal leg brace clattering. George moved nearer to Anna. The music swirling through him, he pictured the places where their bodies touched, the warmth of her hand, the curve of her hip, focusing on them until every nerve of his body turned liquid, a river of wanting flowing toward her. Over her shoulder, he studied a moon dissected into identical squares.

"Anna?" he asked. "You know the stars?"

"Stars? Like movie? Singing? Radio?"

"In the sky. Those stars. Are they the same all over the world? I mean if I'm far away, will they be like they are here or will they be different?"

"They'll be pretty much the same, but I guess it all depends where you go."

"Yeah." He gazed through the meshed windows. "Guess you're right."

The last time he'd been to the armory he was six, the year his father took him to the circus. Whirring calliope music pinged off the metal rafters, and the crowd roared at the wild-haired clowns peddling miniature tricycles. Spangled women waved from atop hopelessly wrinkled elephants while tightrope walkers in silky pants worked without a net. But this morning found the earthy odor of animal cages gone, the tiered bleachers empty, the piping organ replaced by a scowling sergeant barking commands. Draft board nurses in white hats guided the sluggish lines of silent young men through the doctors' stations that circled the armory floor. One doctor placed a stethoscope warmed by the chests of a dozen others over George's heart; another tested his reflexes with the strike of a rubber mallet, a blow that sent his cigarette's dangling ash tumbling to the floor. The doctors' bored eyes never strayed beyond their assigned tasks, and George began to feel like the cow drawing behind the butcher's counter, his body labeled and divided into sections by neat, dotted lines. The armory air grew ripe with sweat, a stink that made Anna seem farther than the ten miles to town.

The night before he left, George and Anna returned to the Bijou. They sat close in the last balcony row, and when the lights dimmed, George reached out for Anna's hand. The newsreel's blaring trumpet cried into the dark. People cheered the first films from the Normandy invasion. George clutched Anna's hand tighter, but even the feel of her so close couldn't provide the anchor for which he'd hoped. The armada of hulking metal ships on the screen formed their own brand of gravity, and deep in his stomach, George surrendered to the will and force of men and machines pulling on him from far across the ocean.

So This is Love

Eric swoops down our unpaved lane, a scene of fury and kicked-up dust not witnessed this side of gladiator movies, his brake lights flashing only when his Camaro bucks to a chassis-squeaking stop. He rushes me into the passenger seat and orders me not to unlock the door for anyone but him. In the moth-fluttering halo of the Camaro's headlights, he fights my stepfather—Eric light on his toes at first, a circling dance of brisk jabs, my stepfather plodding forward, a sadist's grin plastered across his fat mug. Each time my stepfather lands a punch, I cringe, my hands squeezing a purse which contains not only the seven hundred sixty-eight dollars I've saved from my shifts at the supermarket but also the asswipe's wallet. Blood flows. Three times my stepfather knocks Eric down, and three times Eric gets up, a series of wobbly resurrections, his cautious jabs abandoned for wild, grunting haymakers. Finally, the asswipe gives up, spitting on the Camaro's windshield before lumbering back to the house. Eric staggers in the headlights' shine, his knees buckling but his fists still raised. "I'm not licked yet, old man!" he yells. "Not by a fucking long shot!" I help him back into the car, and we speed off. I honk the horn, a final, cursing goodbye to all this drama and small-mindedness, goodbye to my stepfather's precious hunting dogs, their howls and pen-rattling frenzy receding by the time we fishtail onto the road. The speedometer's swift climb testifies to my deliverance from this hell.

141

Silvery clouds shroud the moon, and with the cool, heavy scent of the green fields rushing over us, I know I've never been more alive. I hold a T-shirt to Eric's bloodied face, and the fact that the asswipe has busted my boyfriend's nose matters less than knowing that Eric won't stand for anyone, not even a half-drunk bear who outweighs him by a good hundred pounds, cursing me or making me cry or peeking in at me through the bathroom keyhole. When I show him my stepfather's wallet, Eric tosses it out the window, saying he wouldn't take a million dollars from the jerk-off. This is my kind of love, a two-fisted and bloody adoration, the kind of love people write songs about. The kind of love people die for.

With a twist of his chin, Eric works his face away from the sopping T-shirt. "You didn't tell me he could punch like a mother fucker, honey," he says in an airy, pinched voice.

I put my lips on his and kiss him. The gearshift stabs my ribs. Our wheels veer onto the shoulder, the gravel pinging beneath us in a hundred chunky notes. Blood coats our tongues with its coppery taste. "You are something else," Eric laughs when I pull away. I settle back into my seat and place a hand over the thumb-sized baby floating inside my belly. The night road hums beneath our speeding tires, our car a God-sent chariot taking us anywhere, anywhere but here.

Bad Monkey

A single floodlight shone down from the rectory's roof. Parker had selected this spot last evening, believing the illumination and the proximity of dreaming nuns would deter the thieves who sometimes prowled the midway's fringe. Sitting in the van's opened side door, Parker rubbed cold cream onto his cheeks then wiped off the goo with a paper towel. From the other side of the rectory came the call of hammers and the rumble of small engines. In a few hours, the midway's tent city and clattering rides would slip off into another summer night. Parker held his cell and listened again to his mother's message wishing him a happy twenty-fifth birthday.

He grabbed his ex's seashell-bordered hand mirror. Makeup splotches surely lingered near his hairline and ears, but the light didn't allow him a proper view. He jockeyed the mirror and turned his chin. His reflection passed like moon phases in the glass. The clack of booted footsteps broke his concentration. Two murky figures approached him, their shadows stretching far across the macadam.

Parker tossed the mirror into the van and stood to greet Bartos and Janak Sedlak. Cloaked by the darkness, Janak's acne-scarred cheeks didn't come into focus until he stood close enough for Parker to smell the vodka on his breath. Bartos, thick-chested and sullen, stood slightly behind his brother. The spotlight's glaring cusp shone on Bartos's shaved head. Earlier in the evening, tempers had flared at the Sedlak brothers' midway booth. Fists had been raised, violence threatened, a nerve-racking confrontation Parker defused by suggesting they meet behind the rectory after the brothers had dismantled their stand.

"Sorry about all this," Parker said. His offered hand disappeared in the smothering embrace of Bartos's paw, and his knuckles cracked in Janak's callused grip. The brothers pulled away and examined their palms with disgust.

"It's cold cream." Parker handed each a paper towel. "Sorry."

"You say sorry a lot." Janak wiped his hands and returned the bundled mass to Parker.

"I do," Parker said. The reserve of stage-presence bravery he'd mustered now dwindled beneath Janak's stare. "A habit I guess. Sorry."

Janak tugged his cauliflower ear and turned to his brother. "Again with the sorrys." Janak's flat, guttural tone owed as much to South Chicago as it did to Prague. Parker assumed Bartos possessed the same accent, but he had yet to hear the larger man speak. Bartos tossed Parker his used towel, but Parker fumbled the catch.

Carnivals such as the one he'd just finished comprised a good quarter of Parker's working calendar, but despite his familiarity with this nomadic subculture, Parker remained intimidated by men like Janak and Bartos. In their presence, smelling of a clown's cold cream, Parker couldn't help seeing himself cast in the role of the foolish dandy, a hothouse flower destined to wither in this climate of uncouth men.

Parker offered Janak a slim fold of bills. "Fifty dollars," Parker announced cheerily. "I think that should cover your damages and then some."

Janak counted the bills and turned to his brother. Bartos shook his head. "Bartos says no," Janak said. "Not enough."

Six softball-sized bowls and four goldfish—that was the extent of the damage rendered by Tolstoy, Parker's white-headed capuchin. Tolstoy had unknotted his leash from a fence post and darted off during Parker's silk-handkerchief routine. Parker gave chase, and along the way, his oversized shoes tromped the midway's peanut shells and crushed paper cups. The monkey appeared in eye-blink glimpses before being swallowed back by the rubbernecking crowds. Children squealed and pointed wildly. Parker, his hunched posture imitating his prey, focused on the leash's trailing handle, a lasso of worn leather, as it snaked between the midway's dizzying parade. In the sawdust behind the corndog stand, he snagged the lasso, but before the leash snapped taut, he heard the shriek of breaking glass.

Like most of the midway's population, the Sedlak brothers brokered little interaction with Parker, a freelancer who hooked up with this particular crew only a few times a season. With his theater degree from Northwestern and his semester in London, Parker was decidedly not one of them. The gathered leash in his hand, he had rushed upon the scene to discover Tolstoy cowering in the booth's rear and the stunned Sedlak brothers just coming to terms with the situation. Janak's flashing eyes turned upon the leash which had forged its damning link between Parker, the frightened monkey, and the damage the animal had wrought. Surrounding Parker's buffoonish shoes spread a constellation of broken glass and a handful of desperately flapping goldfish. "The fish are dying, Daddy!" screamed a little girl who held a lollipop as round as her face.

Bartos pricked his finger on a glass shard trying to rescue one of the fish. The sight of his brother's blood infuriated Janak, and Parker reeled backwards—one, two, three steps—with each chest-poking jab of Janak's finger. "What the fuck're you doing, man?" Janak demanded. Tolstoy hissed. Parker appealed to cooler heads and arranged their meeting, his pacifist's heart fluttering then as it was now.

He cleared his throat. "I think fifty is rather reasonable, Janak."

"You hear those kids crying when they see the dead fish?" Janak asked. "The ones flapping around were bad enough, but when your monkey ate one—"

"In all fairness, Janak, he did spit it out."

Parker flinched with Janak's step forward. "Point is, Mr. Monkeyman, those kids left crying and not paying their money to throw the ping-pong balls."

"Well," Parker chuckled, "it may have been a temporary setback, but I'm sure business quickly rebounded as word circulated. After all, they say there's no such thing as bad publicity."

Before Parker could raise a defensive hand, Janak resumed his finger-poking assault, a series of focused blows delivered to the nook below Parker's clavicle. "I don't know what the fuck you're talking about, Mr. Monkeyman, but I'm betting you know exactly what I'm saying, no?"

"OK, OK." Parker retrieved the pay envelope from his van and handed Janak another ten.

Janak held up the bill, but Bartos only raised his bandaged finger. Janak turned back to Parker with a shrug and an extended palm.

Parker handed over another ten. Tolstoy exited the van and ambled to his owner's side. In his paw, he carried Parker's hand mirror which he raised to contemplate his reflection. The three men studied the monkey, and as if on cue, Tolstoy set down the mirror and executed a trio of back flips, a performance which triggered smiles from Janak and even Bartos.

"He is cute when he's not being a pain in the ass," Janak said.

The two men walked off, silhouettes once again. Their waning shadows chased after them, and their laughter carried back to Parker. Tolstoy tugged at Parker's pant leg, and with bared, yellow teeth, restated his empty-bellied complaints.

Parker stepped onto the balcony outside his fourth-story hotel room. He should have slept in his van again, the mathematics of his week's expenses not adding up, but his uncelebrated birthday had left him feeling entitled to the luxuries of a shower and air conditioning and a bed with clean sheets. Tolstoy dozed in the cage Parker had snuck up the side stairwell.

Above, a sprinkling of stars glimmered dully, the August night thick with humidity and cricket calls. In the near distance, the tide of red and white lights testified to the interstate's restless journeys. Tomorrow he'd rise early and travel to the Evansville Summer Days Festival. Back in the room, Parker knelt beside the cage. Granola flecks spotted the fur around Tolstoy's mouth, and his little sides heaved with the faint rhythms of sleep. The monkey had mastered the cage's flimsy lock, so Parker, working quietly, secured the gate with a length of shoelace before leaving.

In the van, he retrieved the whiskey bottle from beneath his sleeping bag. The swimming pool's black surface cupped the reflections of the hotel's few lit windows. A padlock secured the gate, but the chest-high fence was easily scaled, and Parker, bottle in hand, settled onto one of the plastic lounge chairs. The scent of chlorine hung in the air, and the smell reminded him of the line-dried bed sheets of his youth. His feet out, he turned his back to the hotel and allowed himself to be lulled by the purr of interstate traffic.

A breeze rippled the pool's surface. For the first time in days, Parker felt cool, and the chill testified that summer's heat would soon yield to fall. The whiskey slid down his throat and loosened his knotted muscles. He considered the highway's cars, seeing them not as individual hunks of metal but as components of a greater flow, a human tide drawn to some notion of home via routes either direct or serendipitous. For the past few weeks, he'd been thinking often of home, of the solid center a life should have. He'd been lured into this nomad's existence by the love of a fellow theater major, a woman who'd sold him on the romance of taking their craft to the common man. Six months ago, she vanished, leaving behind a hastily scribbled note, their maxed-out credit card, her seashell mirror, and Tolstoy.

Parker took another sip and shuddered. He could finish his current obligations then shed this life he'd stumbled so blindly into. He'd sell the van and give Tolstoy up for adoption. He'd get a job, a real job. With a bit of luck, he'd discover a new home, perhaps not an immediate dwelling of brick and wood, but a sense of belonging he would carve into the soft tissue of his soul. He thought of his mother's message, and his eyes grew wet when he considered how terribly he missed her tonight. He stood, stumbling slightly before righting himself on the pool's apron.

With the elevator's upward jerk, he dropped the banana he'd retrieved from the van for Tolstoy. Released into the corridor's fluorescent sheen, Parker shuffled along, the room's access card gripped tightly. Home was in his future, and tonight, on a proper bed behind a locked door, he would be reintroduced to what gifts such simple things were. His hand paused before he could swipe his card through the lock, a moment in which he hoped the muffled din wasn't coming from his room.

With a push of the door's handle, Parker stumbled into a scene of senseless upheaval. An ear-splitting ruckus boomed from the TV. His suitcase had been opened, his clothes strewn in haphazard piles. A sauna-like wave singed his lungs. The bedspread lay in a crumpled heap, the coffee carafe smashed, the room lit in the skewed shine of a knocked-over lamp. Parker righted a chair, turned off the TV and the crackling heater. He inspected the cage's gnawed shoelace and the balcony's ripped screen. Tolstoy scampered from beneath the bed and snatched the banana.

Parker lunged for the monkey, but Tolstoy eluded his grasp. They scrambled over the bed, hurdled the drawers Tolstoy had yanked from the bureau. Parker believed he had Tolstoy cornered in the bathroom's shower, but the beast vaulted to the curtain rod and swung to safety. In his harried pursuit, Parker slammed his temple into a towel hook, and he staggered back into the room, cursing and clutching his head. Tolstoy squealed from his perch atop the room's only bed and paused for Parker's full attention before urinating on the exposed sheets.

With a headlong dive, Parker snatched him. Tolstoy squirmed and clawed, but Parker locked him in a straightjacket grip and pinned the monkey to the sopping sheets until the fight ebbed from his body. Parker rose. He laughed at the monkey's helplessness; its expression of panic and uncertainty a small payback for all of his cursed tricks. Tolstoy squirmed, a move Parker countered with a hard squeeze. The monkey gasped, and its frantic heartbeat drummed against Parker's sweaty palms.

Tolstoy wriggled a paw free and clawed Parker's eye. Parker yelped and, half-blind, staggered among the floor's debris. He extended his arms, the monkey howling as it vainly swiped the space between them. A breeze wafted through the balcony door's ripped screen. Parker kicked back the screen, a berth just wide enough to wriggle outside. Cooler here, the room's suffocating heat abandoned, and with the temperature drop, a sense of calm found Parker.

The uneasy peace found Tolstoy as well, and with his little chest heaving, he abandoned his struggle. Parker considered the monkey, the beast set against the backdrop of a dark night and the distant, home-seeking beacons of the highway's headlights. Lost love, lost home, lost years, Parker divined them all in the monkey's wet eyes. With an upward swing, he launched Tolstoy toward the murky stars. For a moment, Parker saw Tolstoy, his stunned expression captured in the light that spilled from the room. Tolstoy's paws clutched the empty air, his tail curling into a question mark before he disappeared without a sound.

A swatch of harsh sunlight fell across Parker's face. Before passing out, he'd stripped the drenched sheets and set them on the balcony, but the room still stank. His fingers tested the swollen skin around his eye. He shuffled to the balcony, and the woozy perspective persuaded him to clutch the rail before peering over the edge. He hadn't noticed the row of trees that lined the lot below, a leafy covering which no doubt concealed Tolstoy's battered body.

After his shower, Parker gathered his clothes, the empty cage, and slunk down the side staircase. He couldn't deny his guilt, but also undeniable was the exhilaration borne of being deeply invested in the moment, a level of engagement Parker found oddly intoxicating. He was scared and ashamed and more than a bit freaked out, yet his chest swelled with a sense of purpose he hadn't possessed for months. Perhaps the journey home needed only a push in the right direction, a bloodletting to sever the ties of a life which would no longer claim him.

Before loading his things in the van, he crossed the lot and inspected the grounds beneath his window. The trees, a string of flowering pears no more than fifteen feet tall, claimed the strip of lawn that separated the hotel from the parking lot. A broken branch and a handful of leaves littered the mulch, but there was no sign of Tolstoy. No doubt the monkey had crawled off to die or had been snatched by a dumpster-sniffing dog, and the fact that he wouldn't have to deal with the carcass relieved Parker.

Satisfied, he returned to the van. In his thoughts, he pared down his act to its one-man basics, a liberating subtraction that fortified his morning's optimism, but in the next moment, a latching on his ankle caused him to cry out, a reflexive shriek that drew the attention of the older couple loading their car in a nearby space. Gazing down, Parker felt himself plunged into a realm of shadows and ghosts, for here was Tolstoy, resurrected from the dead.

The monkey emitted a pained gasp when Parker lifted him. Tolstoy hung limply in Parker's grip, his head drooping forward. Parker placed him in the van, and with a foot-dragging limp, Tolstoy crawled onto Parker's sleeping bag. Parker opened a water bottle and brought it to the monkey's mouth. Tolstoy sipped, grimaced, and sipped some more. Water dribbled from the corners of his mouth, his fur matted and wet. The seashell mirror lay next to Tolstoy, and the glass doubled the image of the monkey's exhausted collapse onto the sleeping bag.

An hour later, Parker reached the Evansville Fairgrounds. The sun, nestled in a sea of cloudless blue, beat down, the landscape blurred and shimmering. The whiteface he applied turned gooey on his sweating brow. He coaxed Tolstoy, who'd dragged himself off the sleeping bag, to eat a few bites of banana. With a final tug and buckle snap, Parker secured his stirrups. His stilts extended from the van's driver's side door, his heels anchored in the drought-wilted weeds, the painted wooden toes pointed up at a jaunty angle. Parker yanked the silky material of his parachute pants up his legs and, with a repositioning wriggle, over his waist. Tolstoy gingerly climbed to the ground, and in the field of parched earth that separated them from the midway's stands, the monkey roamed about, his hitching limp evident but fading as he examined the field's trash specks.

"Here boy," Parker called. The monkey winced as it climbed back into the van. Parker secured a miniature fez atop Tolstoy's head. Tolstoy reached into Parker's costume bag, retrieved a red foam ball, and tenderly speared it over Parker's nose, an act so gentle that Parker had to fight the urge to cry. Parker hooked the fifteen-foot leash to the monkey's collar. He arranged his props in a satchel and slung it over his shoulder. Latching onto the top of the opened door, Parker hoisted himself from the van and found his balance atop his five-foot stilts. He gave the leash a beckoning tug and Tolstoy gingerly lowered himself from the van. The field, with its broken bottles and crushed cans, proved bothersome for Parker, his equilibrium further hindered by the baking sun, his stubborn hangover, and Tolstoy's uncharacteristically sluggish pace.

"A monkey!" shrieked a pigtailed girl when Parker stepped onto the midway.

Parker staked his place near the funnel cake stand. He secured the leash to a clasp on his belt. Tolstoy performed a back flip but stumbled forward after a less-than-graceful landing. The crowd grew. The children reached up, their sugar-coated hands grasping as Parker released the balloons he'd blown up and knotted. The animal shapes drifted down in gentle, thoughtless paths.

Parker pulled three apples from his satchel and began to juggle, a beginner's sleight of hand made difficult by Tolstoy's clothing-tugging ascent to Parker's shoulder. "Good boy," Parker whispered. The children roared as Tolstoy snatched one of the apples and chomped a chunk-splattering bite. Parker studied the crowd and smiled. What a gift he'd been granted, Tolstoy's survival rescuing his master from ending this period of his life with an act of blind brutality, and Parker vowed that in its place, he would fill these final months with compassion for the beast that had so often vexed him. When the apple had been eaten to its core, Tolstoy tossed it back into the mix and snared another. Parker's well-rehearsed scoldings only heightened the crowd's reaction. They continued the trick until Parker found himself juggling three cores, which he then deftly tossed, one at a time, into a nearby metal drum.

Tolstoy scampered back down, but before Parker could pull his ukulele from his bag, a commotion erupted. The pigtailed girl yelped, and the crowd to Parker's right pulled back, a rippling, shared reflex. Parker glanced down to discover Tolstoy feverishly stuffing a hotdog bun into his mouth. A thick-chested man waved a finger at Parker. "You're going to pay for that hotdog, mister!"

Parker's apology was cut short by a sharp tug on his belt. His arms waved, a momentary rebalancing. Tolstoy, a pilfered candy apple in hand, darted behind Parker. A little boy with caramel-glazed lips bawled. "Get that monkey out of here!" snapped the woman who scooped up the crying boy and clutched him against her chest. "He's a menace!"

The circle around Parker receded while the outer edges thickened with curious passers-by. Tolstoy wrestled away an old woman's purse. Prescription vials and an eyeglass case clattered to the ground, a mess swiftly carpeted by a box of spilled popcorn. Helium balloons released in surprise dwindled to colored specks, pinpoints swallowed by the ocean-wide sky.

Parker fumbled to unlock the clasp attached to his belt and reel in Tolstoy, but the leash, now wrapped Maypole-like around his stilts, offered no slack. Tolstoy continued his possessed lurchings, scampering around Parker in ever-decreasing orbits, the leash pulled tighter and tighter. Another jerk, and Parker teetered, his hips swaying in countering thrusts as Tolstoy attempted to snare a half-eaten corndog that had been dropped onto the macadam.

The stilts' height added to the suspended moments of Parker's fall, a pregnant breath in which he sensed the false security of such a beautiful day. There was the unbothered blue above, and all around him, the fair's array of bright colors and sweet aromas and breeze-ruffled flags. Below, on the unforgiving and rapidly approaching macadam, Tolstoy danced an anticipating jig. His leathery paws clapped with excitement, and his thin lips crinkled into a knowing grin.

About the Author

CURTIS SMITH is the author of five previous books of fiction. 2010 will see the release of his next novel and his first essay collection. His stories and essays have appeared in over fifty literary journals and have been cited by *The Best American Short Stories, The Best American Mystery Stories,* and *The Best American Spiritual Writing.* He lives and works in Pennsylvania with his wife and son.

About the Cover Artists

ANGUS DUNICAN is a performer and writer and one time photo model. Prior to attending Goldsmiths College to study drama and theatre arts, he self produced and co-wrote two shows for the Edinburgh Fringe Festival and enjoyed a career as a stand-up comic. He has also sung lead tenor with the Glyndebourne Youth Opera and occasionally teaches physical theatre to under 12s. Recently, he began investigating installation art and produced his first piece, "Represented Here..." at the Shunt Lounge (London Bridge) in collaboration with his friend and fellow artist Nicola Block (2008). He lives and works in London.

MURRAY BALLARD is a photographer born and based in Brighton, UK. He graduated from the University of Brighton in 2007 with a First Class degree in Editorial Photography. In June 2008 he was selected by The Photographers Gallery in London for their Fresh Faced and Wild Eyed 08 exhibition, a showcase of the most dynamic new work by visual arts graduates across the UK. His work has also been shown at the Host Gallery, London, in the FOTO8 Summer Show 08, and was exhibited in the Brighton Photo Festival in October 2008. His photography has been published nationally and internationally in several journals and magazines, including the prestigious *FOTO8* and *YVI* magazines.

His current practice is concerned with documenting cutting-edge scientific research and experimentation that has the potential to shape and define our future. He is currently working on the project "The Prospect of Immortality," an investigation into the scientific technology used in preserving the dead—for possible revival in the future; and he is about to begin a new project on bioengineering at The John Innes Centre in Norwich, UK.

.